GAGE

SMOKEJUMPERS

BOOK FOUR

BY EVIE RILEY

Gage

Smokejumpers

Book Four

Copyright © 2024

Evie Riley

Second Edition

ISBN: 978-1-77357-682-4

Published by Naughty Nights Press LLC

Cover Art By Willsin Rowe

GAGE

One stormy night could change everything...

Firefighter Gage Torres is currently certified to work the rescue squad and perform dangerous rescues on shift, but his adrenaline junkie side is always looking for more. Recently chosen for the coveted opportunity to become trained to work forest fires, he's excited to ship out to California and get started. Only thing is, he has to leave his younger brothers behind, whom he's never been away from, but they have some unexpected news of their own to share.

Aerial Firefighter Xavier Cruz is an instructor for the Sacramento Fire Division. Rough around the edges, Xavier prefers to remain a loner. He doesn't have close friends, his social skills are terrible, and even his sixteen-year-old son doesn't like him. A former fighter pilot for the Air Force, he suffers from PTSD and has turned to alcohol to fight the nightmares. But if he's ever going to mend his relationship with his son to protect him like a real father would, Xavier needs to find a way to get sober, and fast.

During a routine practice flight, their helicopter is attacked and they crash in the forest. With no map and no cell signal, the men must find a way to survive both a storm and crazy extremists with no supplies until they can get to safety. Forced to share body heat when they spend the night in a cave, things take an unexpected turn and survival becomes a night neither of them can seem to forget.

Will Gabe and Xavier make the connection between them work, or are they doomed from the start?

CHAPTER ONE

Gage

I SANK INTO the worn leather chair, the familiar creak echoing through the firehouse's morning haze. The room, dimly lit by the soft glow of emergency exit signs and flickering overhead lighting, carried the aroma of stale coffee and lingering solidarity. The worn wooden table before me bore the scars of countless debates, laughter, and the occasional game of poker.

Around me, my fellow firefighters sprawled in various states of fatigue, nursing mugs of coffee like lifelines. The room hummed with the low buzz of conversation, punctuated by the occasional raucous laughter. The worn-out radio crackled intermittently, its static-filled messages a constant reminder of the unpredictable nature of our calling. Captain Clarke's distinctive voice reached my ears, a steady undercurrent in the background as I waited for the morning check-in meeting to officially commence.

I watched as every member of the group walked in and proceeded to approach Jase, welcoming him back into the fold with back slapping and a general happiness to have him return. The team spirit was palpable, a tangible force that bound us together in a brotherhood forged by flames and shared risks. The banter flowed effortlessly, seasoned with firefighting jargon as my teammates described their recent call outs and the gallows humor that was our coping mechanism for the relentless stress of our profession.

I leaned back in my chair, absorbing the banter as the room gradually settled into a semblance of order. I drummed my fingertips absentmindedly on the tabletop, a silent rhythm mirroring the pulse of anticipation coursing through my veins this morning.

Captain Clarke strode to the front, his presence demanding immediate attention from everyone in the room. His weathered face betrayed the countless battles he'd fought alongside us, etched with lines that spoke of both victories and losses. The room hushed, the collective gaze fixed on the man who held our destinies in his calloused hands.

"All right, listen up, everyone," Captain Clarke's gravelly voice cut through the air. The room fell silent, every eye trained on our leader. "First let me say, welcome back, Turner. It's been quiet around here without you."

"Thanks, Cap," Jase responded. "It's good to be back. I'm sure you all had a difficult time around here without my bright and sunny disposition to keep you going." He flashed his pearly whites and then ducked his head.

Gaffaws and chuckles, and slow motion clapping rang out in the room before the commotion died down and the captain continued. He delved into the details of the previous day's incidents, the lessons learned, and the challenges faced. The air crackled with a mixture of focused attention and the shared understanding that each word could be a nugget of wisdom crucial for survival.

As Captain Clarke transitioned into the plan for the day ahead, my senses sharpened. The distant wail of sirens outside, the rhythmic thud of boots on the linoleum floor, the acrid scent of turnout gear—all familiar elements that composed the symphony of a firehouse morning.

And then, he dropped the long-anticipated bombshell.

"We've got an opening for the aerial firefighters division in Sacramento, California," Captain Clarke announced, and a hush fell over the room. My heart quickened its pace, anticipation and anxiety intertwining in a chaotic dance. My mind whirled and I sent up a quick prayer.

Please say it. Tell me I've finally been chosen.

"And," he continued, locking eyes with me, "Torres, pack your bags and make whatever arrangements you need to. You'll be wheels up tomorrow at oh eight hundred."

A stunned silence enveloped me, broken only by the sounds of the firehouse waking up to a new day. The weight of the announcement settled on my shoulders, a mix of exhilaration and trepidation.

My fellow firefighters erupted into cheers, clapping me on the back and offering hearty congratulations. The room transformed into a cacophony of laughter and excitement, and amidst it all, I felt a surge of pride. The coveted training, a chance to soar through the skies and battle blazes from above, was now within my grasp. Finally.

As the reality sank in, I couldn't help but crack a grin. I'd been chosen for a placement that transcended the routine of life here at the station, a chance to elevate my skills to new heights.

The room continued to buzz with excitement, and I found myself caught in a whirlwind of congratulations and well wishes. My fellow firefighters, Hawke, Jase, Johnson, Zander, Carmen, Mark, Cy, and Quinn, our weekly rotated paramedics Newt and Ellie, each one a brother or sister in arms, surrounded me, offering slaps on the back and words of encouragement. The air was charged with energy, and I couldn't help but feel a surge of pride and gratitude for the friendships that bound us together even beyond the firehouse.

Amidst the elation, I exchanged nods and smiles with my colleagues, their genuine happiness reflecting the tight-knit bond forged through countless shared experiences. Captain Clarke, his eyes crinkling at the corners with a rare smile, approached me with a firm handshake.

"Torres, you've earned this opportunity. Make us proud up there," he said, his words carrying the weight of both expectation and trust.

"Thank you, Captain. I won't let you down," I replied, the gravity of the moment settling in.

As the room gradually quieted, Captain Clarke regained control of the meeting, transitioning into the nitty-gritty details of the day's assignments and ongoing projects. My mind, however, raced ahead, already envisioning the challenges and adventures that awaited me in the aerial firefighters division.

The morning sunlight streamed through the grimy windows, casting a warm glow on the firehouse memorabilia that adorned the walls. The familiar scent of old leather and fire-resistant fabric hung in the air, a comforting reminder of the home I was about to leave behind temporarily.

The next day flashed in my mind like a series of rapid-fire images—the airport hustle, the hum of the plane's engines, and the anticipation of stepping onto unfamiliar ground. I couldn't suppress the mix of nerves and excitement that surged through me. This was a chance to push my limits, to evolve as a firefighter, and to contribute to missions that transcended the boundaries of the firehouse.

As the meeting drew to a close, the room gradually emptied, each firefighter dispersing to tackle the day's tasks. I remained seated for a moment longer, absorbing the gravity of the moment. The journey ahead promised growth, challenges, and the opportunity to make a difference on a larger scale.

I rose from the worn leather chair, a sense of purpose coursing through my veins. The firehouse, once a familiar sanctuary, now felt like the launching pad for a new chapter. I exchanged more nods and encouraging words with my coworkers as I made my way toward the gear room to prepare for the day ahead.

The journey to California loomed on the horizon, a path filled with unknowns and possibilities. I couldn't help but reflect on the journey that led me to this point—the countless drills, the shared laughter and hardships, and the unwavering support of my firefighting family, and my reason for it all.

My younger brothers, Greyson and Asher.

With a deep breath and a sense of determination similar to the one that had seen me through many life challenges so far, I welcomed the new opportunities that lay ahead. I was so ready to soar into the skies and face the flames from a new perspective.

CHAPTER TWO

Xavier

BEEP... BEEP... BEEP...

I smacked my hand down on the annoying alarm clock next to my bed with a groan. I was not ready to be awake right now. I was not ready to face the headache that I knew would hit me the second my eyes opened.

I hated Mondays. I hated most days,

but Mondays were the worst. I wasn't a morning person. Shit, I wasn't even an afternoon person. I was a night owl. I preferred to be up all night and sleep during any sunlight hour, especially if that meant I could avoid the hustle and bustle of people all over the place.

I didn't mind being around crowds when it was in a bar, when I could drink and find the next guy to have a one-night stand with. But when I had to be sober during the day and in a crowd, I always felt like my skin was crawling. Something as simple as walking down a busy street was difficult and the act of grocery shopping during peak hours, fucking forget about it. Being around people was hard, especially idiots.

There were times when I was at work and I had to go off and be by myself because I couldn't handle the stupidity and immaturity that some of the others have. I knew it was part of life, that at some point I was just as stupid as them, but I wasn't at that part of my life anymore. I couldn't handle most things that I used to be able to. And I knew that was from the PTSD.

Fuck, I was so sick of hearing those four letters.

I had been in the Air Force since I was eighteen. I enlisted right on my eighteenth birthday and I didn't regret it, not for a single second. Yes, shit had been hard plenty of times and there were an endless number of close calls over the years, but my time in service had been some of the best years of my life. I had made some of the strongest bonds that could be possible. They were all dead now, which hurt, but I didn't ever regret knowing them, even if that meant I had to deal with the hurt of burying them.

I had been honorably discharged four years ago when I was thirty-eight. It was a bit by choice and a bit forced, but that's a story I try never to think about. The shrink that I was forced to see before starting my new job told me I had PTSD, but it would only affect my personal life and not my professional life so I was cleared to keep flying planes.

I didn't believe the whole PTSD thing at first. I thought it was bullshit and just some fancy way to say I get nightmares.

Who the fuck wouldn't have nightmares after what I'd seen?

Turns out, she might have been on to something because as time went on, I started to notice different things. Like how life was so much easier if I was drunk for most of it. Obviously, I never drank when I was working or on call, but when I was free to do whatever I wanted, I spent most of it drunk. It also destroyed my desire to be social, which put my social skills down to questionable at best.

The thing was though, I didn't give a shit. I didn't care to be social and happy all of the time. I didn't care to listen to pathetic little problems that people complained about like they were something serious. I couldn't listen to people going on and on about their coworkers or being cheated on. I had to scrape my friends up off of the ground with a shovel and put them into buckets.

Why the fuck would I care about someone's boyfriend not being able to keep it in his pants?

If that made me anti-social, then I was more than happy to be. You couldn't tell that to a Shrink though, they'd just tell you that you had survivor's guilt and deep-rooted traumas that were masked by sarcasm. And maybe they were, or maybe I was just an old, bitter cat who wanted to be left the fuck alone.

What was so wrong with that?

Seriously, I wasn't hurting anyone with how I was. I wasn't in a relationship. I didn't bring any toxic behavior around people.

If I didn't want to be happy and social, then why did it matter to other people?

I was content with the way that I was and that should have been good enough.

There was one regret in my life, fuck many, but the biggest regret would be my ex-wife. Sure, most people felt that way about their ex-spouse, I knew she did about me as well. The thing was though, I regretted ever kissing her, let alone marrying her. At the same time though, it was a double edge sword, because if I hadn't kissed her, if I hadn't married her, I wouldn't have my son Dexter. He was the only pride and joy that I had. The only one who could truly bring a smile to my face.

When I'd discovered that Kate was pregnant almost seventeen years ago, I had never felt so happy before in my life. I never thought I would have children and then I found out I was having a son. I couldn't have been happier. I was there for everything. Every doctor's appointment, every ultrasound, all of the food cravings, the decorating, everything. I was hands-on and there for it all and when he was born, it was me who cut his umbilical cord. I was the one who held him first.

The very second that I held him in my arms I was in love. The feeling of seeing him, of getting to hear his cry, there was no other feeling like it in the world. There was no way to describe it. It was an instant tidal wave of love, a drive to keep him safe and give him the best life that I possibly could. Even if that meant I had to stay with his mother and continue to keep my true desires a secret. I would do anything that I could to give him the best life.

I grew up with amazing parents. They had been together since they were in high school and they were madly in love until the day they died. They never fought in front of me. They were always affectionate with each other. If one was sick or tired, the other was there for them. If one was sad, the other comforted them. If one was happy, they were both happy. Their love was pure and contagious and I wanted that for my son. I wanted him to grow up seeing love and happiness between his parents.

I had tried my best. I pushed down my desires and urges to be with a man. I continued to live a life in the closet and foolishly believed that I could be with my wife and be happy. That the sex could be satisfying if I only tried harder. I was delusional and that delusion was ultimately the end of our happy life.

The end of normalcy for Dexter.

For six years we were the perfect family. I was often gone from operations and deployment, but we made it work. I had to give it to Kate, she was the perfect military wife. She never complained about having to relocate with literally thirty days notice. She never complained when I was called away at any given time of the day or night, including birthdays, holidays, and anniversaries. She never freaked out if I came home a bit injured. She was the ideal military wife and the men all envied what I had. They envied not having arguments with their spouse. They envied the type of mother she was. They envied how easy it was.

What they didn't see was that I was dying inside.

I loved Dexter and I wanted everything for him, but every single kiss that Kate gave me, every time we touched, I felt like an enemy was touching me. It made my skin crawl. It made me sick just thinking about being with her sexually and it was wrong. I knew it was wrong to feel that way, to put her through it, but I couldn't help it. I couldn't tell her that I wasn't attracted to her, that I was attracted to men. She didn't sign up for that.

I knew I was gay when I first kissed her when I was sixteen. I knew I wasn't attracted to her, but back then there was no such thing as acceptable homosexuality. You didn't broadcast it and if you wanted to survive high school, you had to fit within a specific box. It was just supposed to be to get me through high school and then I would be in the Air Force and we would go our separate ways.

Only, she was supportive of my decision to be in the military. She was in love with me and the military was even less accepting of homosexuals, so I continued to play along. When we had been together for years, it was natural to propose to her and get married. If I had died in action, she deserved to have the benefits. She had been in my life long enough and put up with me, she had earned the widow benefits. Then Dexter came along and it all snowballed, all from a single kiss back in high school.

For six years after my son was born we made it work, but one afternoon, the one time I had given in to temptation, my whole life changed. It was an afternoon and Dexter was at school, Kate was supposed to be out with her friends until that evening. I was supposed to be alone, so when I invited a man that I had found on a sex app over for some afternoon fun, I figured we would be fine.

At that point, I had never been with a

man before. I just wanted to see just once what it felt like. I wanted to feel like myself for just one afternoon and it was amazing. The second our lips touched, I knew exactly what I had been missing. It was like a dream come true.

Until Kate walked in on us having sex in our bed.

In that one instant my entire life changed and my son's entire life changed. I had hoped after Kate had calmed down that we could talk about it. That I could finally be honest with her and we would work through it. That we could have an amicable divorce and co-parent like civil adults.

Only that wasn't what happened.

Kate had grown up in a very religious family. I knew that and in hindsight she really was the worst girl for me to kiss or marry, but it was far too late to change anything. She demanded that I go to conversion therapy, but that wasn't something that I could do. I was gay, and despite not being out and proud, I wasn't going to sit and listen to someone telling me that I needed to be cured from a disease.

I didn't have a disease. I had a closet problem.

When I refused, she had left. I thought she would be gone for the night and then calm down. I was spun up that night and when I returned three days later, all of her and Dexter's things were gone and she had already filed for divorce and sole custody. I wasn't going to give her sole custody of Dexter. I wanted joint custody, at least, and I fought through court for it, but with being deployed and getting spun up at a moment's notice, the judge granted Kate full custody and left visitation up to her.

Kate had not calmed down over the weeks or months that followed her finding me in bed with another man. She often kept Dexter from me and refused to allow me to see him. She was convinced I would *infect* him.

What the fuck?

I had to watch as my son grew up through social media and photos. Whenever I called, she wouldn't answer. Whenever I sent gifts, they would be returned to me. She would move and not tell me where they were living.

On the rare occasions that I could see Dexter, it was hard. Dexter had grown distant from me, especially during his teenage years. I didn't blame him. I knew that Kate would often tell him that I didn't care enough to be there. She put it all on me and not on her own actions.

Now he was sixteen, almost seventeen, and he didn't really want anything to do with me. He was angry all the time and he didn't like me. I was the *deadbeat dad* in his life and that wasn't what I wanted for him.

This wasn't the life that I wanted for him.

I hadn't told him the full story. He believed that I cheated on Kate, which was true, but he thought it was with a woman. I was scared to tell Dexter the truth, because he grew up with Kate and her family. He went to church every week and she constantly pushed her religious beliefs onto him. I didn't know how he would react if he discovered I was gay. I didn't want to risk losing him and I was terrified that I would if he knew I was gay.

All I could do was try to be there for him and hope that in time he would see that I wanted to be there and it was his mother who had kept me from him.

Even after Kate discovered I was gay, I still kept it a secret. I would meet up for a quick booty call from a sex app, but I was very much in the closet. I couldn't come out, not with being in the military. The guys that I worked with wouldn't understand.

That did change though, once I was discharged.

I figured I was at a point in my life where I wouldn't have to keep that part of myself a dirty secret. I wasn't walking in any parade, but I wasn't hiding in a dark underground club either. I still hadn't dated anyone, just kept it to one night stands or the few fuck buddies that I had. Friends with benefits would be putting it a bit generously.

I didn't like hanging out with them, or even pillow talk. I just wanted sex and for them to leave, it was just that simple to me. I had problems, I knew that, and it wasn't fair to drag anyone into my problems. They were my problems that I got from being in war. I had made the choice to go, and it wasn't fair to make someone else take on my problems for decisions I had made.

My phone's alarm going off only reminded me that I was supposed to be getting up. I let out a groan, as I reached over and finally opened my eyes to turn it off. The second my eyes opened, that headache that I knew would be hitting me, hit me.

That was the downside to drinking. The morning after when that hangover hits you, it was a serious bitch. I couldn't roll over and go back to sleep, even though I really wanted to. Just like I couldn't have a shot of whiskey for the hair of the dog, because I had to be prepared to fly if I should need to.

After I got out of the Air Force I didn't know what I wanted to do, but I knew I wanted to continue to fly. I had moved out to Sacramento, California, my hometown, and joined the fire department as an aerial firefighter. I was the guy who flew the planes or choppers to help when there was a forest fire. I would bring water with specialty planes and I would fly with firefighters or paramedics for search and rescue. It was different compared to flying over a war zone. There was a simplicity to it, but it still allowed me to utilize my skills.

There was also a personal connection to helping with stopping forest fires.

My parents had been killed in a forest fire twenty years ago in Northern California. They were on a camping trip when a forest fire broke out from a lightning strike during a storm. I had been on tour at the time and when the call came in, I didn't even know what to do or to think. I had lost both of them completely out of the blue. I didn't have any siblings and both of my grandparents were dead. They had died when I was younger.

Having to bury my parents, it was a surreal experience, one that to this day still didn't feel real. I was still waiting to see their name pop up on my phone when it rang. I honestly didn't think I would ever get used to them not being in my life. Not being on the other end of the phone. Losing them, it made me want to keep helping people and with being an aerial firefighter, I could do just that.

I had worked forest fires all over Northern California, Texas, and in Montana. Wherever it was needed, we went, and we did everything we could to help save lives.

Today, I was supposed to be helping to get ready for some new recruits to be here tomorrow. We ran different training courses to turn normal firefighters into aerial firefighters. We were always in need of more firefighters to help with the forest fires.

Forest fires were twice as deadly as a

standard fire and they often took a lot longer to put out. When a fire was in a building, it could only burn as long as there was fuel for it. Eventually, it would run out of fuel once the building was gone. That wasn't the case with a forest fire, because there was always fuel for the fire. Whether that was the trees, the grass, the log cabins in the forest or the cities that were close by. There was always something the fire could eat to keep going that made it very difficult to completely put out. It was why some forest fires could take weeks to completely put out and it was grueling on the firefighters.

My job was to make sure they got in and out safely and I provided air support with the water bombers. I also had to keep track of the fire and predict which way it was going to move based on the destruction speed of the fire and wind direction. I was their eyes and it was a job that I took very seriously and I expected all of the firefighters on the ground to do the same.

I wasn't a fan of teaching, but I was one of the harder instructors and everyone knew that if I said one of the guys was good, that meant they were good and they could trust that person with their lives. It was why I was so hard on the cadets. A lot of lives rested on their shoulders and I would be the one to make sure they were ready to handle it.

The ding from my phone telling me I had a new text message only made me groan once again. We had a lot of work to get finished today before the new cadets arrived tomorrow and I wasn't looking forward to it.

I pushed myself up and instantly regretted it. Once again it felt like my brain was trying to escape through my eye sockets. Sitting up on my bed for a moment, I took the time to check out the damage to my studio apartment. I knew if a Shrink ever stepped foot in here they would immediately make me see them four times a week. I had empty beer bottles and whiskey bottles all over the place. Along with take out containers and pizza boxes.

The furniture in my place left something to be desired. I only had my bed, a double mattress and box spring on the floor, an old loveseat, an old coffee table that by some miracle was still standing, and my tv. Other than that, I had some clothes in a duffle bag and that was it. I didn't have any photos up, nothing personal at all. This was a studio apartment, not a home. I didn't know how to make it a home. I didn't know if I wanted a home.

I knew I should want more. I should want a nice place that was home to me. I knew that, I did, but I couldn't seem to bring myself to care to make it happen. Some days by the time I made it through work I was so exhausted that I couldn't even string two words together, much less figure out how to make my place look like a mentally stable person lived there. I knew I had to figure it out, but I couldn't bring myself to care enough to even get started on figuring out how to do that. I certainly wasn't going to start now. I had to get to work and maybe tonight I might have enough energy to think about it. I doubted it, though.

CHAPTER THREE

Gage

"YOU'RE SERIOUSLY DROPPING this shit on me now?"

Holy fuck, I loved my brothers, I did, but they both had the worst timing for when they told me shit. Part of that was my fault, I was man enough to admit it, but in my defense I was young when I had to step up and raise them and they did not make it easy for me.

At eighteen, I should have been a free man. Free to explore the world and build my own life, but instead I found myself raising identical twin eleven-year-old boys. It wasn't our mother's fault, she didn't plan on getting cancer and she sure as shit didn't plan on dying a week after I turned eighteen. At least she hung on that long so the twins wouldn't end up in foster care, but sometimes I wondered if maybe they would have been better off if they did end up in a loving two parent household.

It wasn't easy growing up, far from it. I loved my mother, but she was a single mother for most of my life. My father took off the second that stick turned blue, and to this day I still had never met him. I wouldn't know him if he was standing right in front of me. It was just my mother and me for the first seven years of my life. Then my mother met the twins' father and he stuck around until they were five. He was the twins' father, but he wasn't mine. He wasn't even interested in being a stepfather. Shit, he wasn't all that interested in being a father to the twins.

When he took off I was twelve and had to take on a huge responsibility with taking care of the twins when my mother had to go back to work. It was on me to get the twins to school. It was on me to make sure they got home from school. It was on me to make sure any homework was done. It was on me to cook dinner for all four of us. It was on me to make sure they were bathed and in bed at a decent hour. At twelve years old, I was raising two five-year-old boys while our mother worked all day or all night long to make enough money to keep a roof over our heads or food on our table.

It was hard. There were plenty of days where I was exhausted and didn't know if I could do it. The days where all three of us had the flu and I had to still take care of them while being sick, because even one day off for our mother could mean we didn't eat one day.

That was our life until I was fourteen and she started to get sick. She was rundown all the time, not eating, losing weight, she always had a headache, and she woke up with new bruises with no idea of where they came from. One day, she collapsed at work and was taken to the hospital. We found out she had blood cancer; stage three.

I could still remember the look on the

twins' faces when I had to tell them that our mother was sick. When they asked me if she was going to die, all I could tell them was no, even though I was terrified that she was. She fought with everything in her. She continued to work as often as she could, even while going through chemotherapy and radiation.

I couldn't work until I was fifteen and then I picked up a part-time job at a restaurant as a busboy. It was incredibly hard though, having to balance working, school, and the twins. Plus being there for my mother during her treatments and taking care of her when she was sick.

I had to do it all though, because if anyone suspected that something was going on we would have been taken away from her. Child Protective Services would have been called and then we all would have been split up and placed in foster care.

That wasn't what I wanted.

I had friends at school who were in foster homes and it was horrific. I wasn't going to risk that happening to the twins or myself. So I pushed through and I raised them and took care of my mother. For four years we made it work, until she lost her fight against cancer.

When the social worker showed up after her funeral, she asked me if I was going to have custody of the twins, I hesitated. It wasn't because I didn't love them, it was because I was exhausted. I had been going non-stop since I was twelve and I was just worn out and wanted to have the chance to have a normal life. I told myself they could go to a loving home together. That they would never split twins up. But then every story that I had heard from my friends popped into my head and I knew that I couldn't roll the dice on their lives. I had to take them, because they were safe with me.

It'd been just us ever since and I had joined the Fire Academy as a way to provide for them. At the time there was no waitlist to get in, and I knew it would be a good paycheck for someone that only had a high school diploma, and just barely. I would have health benefits for all three of us, plus dental. The dental was huge because they both needed braces at the time. Becoming a firefighter was all about giving the three of us a chance at a decent life.

Now they were eighteen and how were they paying me back for all of the years of sacrifice I'd made?

By surprising me with life-altering decisions two hours before I was supposed to be on a plane to fly out to Sacramento, California.

Fuck me.

"You asked us what we wanted to do once we graduated," Asher replied, shrugging a shoulder.

Asher was the older twin, by all of ninety-three seconds, and he never let Greyson forget it. Though, Greyson liked to point out that he was smarter, to which Asher always countered that Greyson was only smarter because he stood on Asher's head for a good three months before they were born. The two of them were identical by looks, right down to the fucking smattering of freckles on their faces. Honestly, sometimes I still got confused on who was who. In my defense though, they liked to switch places.

Asher was terrible at school, especially math, so Greyson used to go and sit in his math class to take his tests. The teachers either never noticed or they were too tired and overworked to care. Either way, the only reason Asher had graduated high school at all was because of Greyson. I knew I should've been angry about it, but I was more relieved than anything.

"I meant for the summer. I meant parties you wanted to go to or a vacation you were looking to take. Not that you wanted to go work at a horse ranch in Texas or for Thing Two to be enlisting in the fucking Army." I ran my hands over my face, forcing back the resulting nervous tension from the bomb they'd just dropped, even as my guts wound into a tight knot.

For fuck's sake, all they had to do was behave while I was gone for the aerial training in California. I was only going to be gone for a month. All they had to do was behave for the last two days of school, really. They'd both graduated and they did the whole walk across the stage and throw the hat thing. The school had done it a few days early because all of the Seniors were supposed to help with an end of school carnival and they didn't want to run the risk of leaving the graduation ceremony too late and some of the Seniors couldn't be there. It worked out great for me, because I got to see them graduate.

"I don't see how it's a big deal. You knew we were going to get jobs and start our own lives," Asher commented.

"I know and I get that you are both

young adults now and want to start your lives. But you have never mentioned your desire to move to another state. To work with horses. Do you even know anything about a horse ranch?" I said to Asher before I turned to Greyson, who was supposed to be my smart brother. "And the Army? Seriously? You know that involves running right? You have to do push ups and sit-ups, you have to run with a hundred pounds on your back. You have to shoot a gun at people."

"I know what the Army does. I am well aware of the physical challenges, but Asher has been helping me and I already passed the physical qualification tests. I think this is more about you coming back in a month to an empty home," Greyson calmly alleged.

"Don't. Don't Shrink talk me. I'm

pissed that you both have clearly known about this for a while now and you didn't tell me. You waited until I was just about out the door before you decided to inform me that when I come home you'll both be in different States. I had the right to know. I had the right to process it all and be involved in that decision making. We don't have secrets, that's the rule. It's been the rule since you were five years old. You tell me everything, even that you both dated the same guy at the same time without telling him. You can tell me that, but you seriously couldn't tell me this before now? Urgh."

And that is what it came down to. They kept something that important a secret from me. As if I would be furious that they wanted to make plans for their lives. It wasn't even that they would be out of the house or in a different State, it was that I didn't get to be there for the planning stage.

We could have taken a trip to Texas to look at different horse ranches to find the right one for Asher to work at. Greyson could have been within ROTC to see if he did in fact want to be in the Army without the complexity of enlisting. I had always been supportive of what they chose to do with their lives. I had always walked that fine line between being a father and their big brother. It wasn't always easy, but I didn't want to give up being their brother in favor of being the parent.

Why leave me out now?

To be honest, it hurt, and I wasn't afraid to let them know it.

I deserved better.

"Look, we're sorry. We didn't know how

you would react. It's all new to us, to all three of us and we didn't want what little time we had left living together to be filled with anger. We just wanted to have fun. But we should have told you," Asher said, his voice contrite.

"It's all new to us. Even Ash and me, we're gonna be in different States. The three of us have always been together and now everything is going to change. We just wanted some normalcy and we didn't want you to worry about us. I was also worried you would be disappointed in me for going into the Army and not medical school," Greyson confessed, his eyes downcast.

"All I want is for you both to be happy and healthy. I thought you were going into medical school, because you're so smart and you've been volunteering at the free clinic for four years now. I thought you wanted to be a doctor. You applied for medical schools and received a full scholarship for Harvard." And that was what I couldn't get over.

Who in their right mind turned down a free ride at one of the best medical schools?

"I want to be an Army Medic. I want to help other soldiers to return alive. I want to be able to help protect people and serve this country. You have been a firefighter for seven years. For seven years we've watched as you risked your life to save other people. I want to do that too, just in a different way."

Fuck.

Leave it to Greyson to guilt trip me without even trying. I rubbed the back of my neck.

"Okay, okay. You both know I love you and you know I will always support you and your decisions. If this is what you both truly want to do and what you want your careers to be, then I will support it and I will always be there for you."

It terrified me that Greyson wanted to join the Army. I had no idea what I was supposed to do with that. How to handle knowing that he would be going into war zones and being shot at and there was nothing I could do to protect him.

I was a protector through and through. It didn't matter if I knew a person or not, if they were in trouble I was going to be there for them. I had been in dozens of fights at the bar for defending a guy who was being harassed for being gay. I was gay myself and I had been out and proud since I was fifteen. I didn't care what other people thought, I was going to be myself and if they didn't like it, then they could kick rocks. I didn't care.

When the twins told me they were gay at fourteen, I was a bit surprised.

I mean, what were the odds?

But it did make things a lot easier in terms of giving them the sex talk. Helping them with their relationships was a hell of a lot easier.

Now they were both going to be starting their own lives in two different States and I would have to deal with not seeing them every day. I was going to be alone for the first time in twenty-five years. I wasn't going to have to come home from work and help with homework. I wasn't going to have to make breakfast or dinner for all of us every night. There wouldn't be any movie marathons on the weekend. No more nights where we would sit outside and barbecue and go for a swim. No more birthday parties or pool parties. Even Christmas or Thanksgiving, if they both couldn't get time off it was just going to be me. I had no idea how I was going to handle that. How I was going to handle the quiet.

"We know you will and we love you too," Greyson said, flashing me a warm smile.

"How come you didn't think I would be a doctor?" Asher said, effectively ruining the sweet moment between us all.

"Seriously?" Greyson asked with a smirk.

"You know I love you, but you are the farthest thing from book smart, Ash. I honestly thought you were never going to move out. That you would be an unemployed model until you gained too much weight and started to work at a burger joint," I teased, following with a slight chuckle.

It sounded wrong, I knew that, but he wasn't book smart. Greyson was the book smart brother and Asher was the street smart brother. He knew people, he knew how to survive in the world. I teased him all the time about being a pretty face, but he knew that I loved him and I was only joking. I figured he would actually work in construction or be a personal trainer. Him going to work on a horse ranch fit him perfectly, in fact, and I truly hoped he had an amazing time doing it and it was something he loved.

"You're such an asshole," Asher said, flashing me a warm smile.

We all laughed at that. I could

sometimes be an asshole. I was hardheaded and anyone who knew me would tell you that. It was a result of having to grow up so fast. I wasn't used to asking for help. I was used to being the one that had to give help. A lot of that was because we couldn't ask for help growing up because then the authorities would come knocking and we all risked being split up. I had to handle everything myself, no matter how hard things got.

The guys at work called me the Reckless Brother. I loved riding my motorcycle, skydiving, bungee jumping, anything that had to do with adrenaline, I was all for it. It was why I wanted to learn how to be a Smokejumper and fight forest fires. I loved being a firefighter. Something that I started because it was my best chance at providing for the twins. I never expected to fall in love with it, but I did and I fell hard. I couldn't imagine doing anything else with my life and that's what I wanted for the twins. I wanted them to love their job and be excited to go to work every day.

"I love you too. Do you both have everything you need? Do you know where you're living?" I had to leave to go to the airport soon, but I needed to make sure they were both set for their new adventures or if I needed to help them get things figured out before they left.

"I'll be staying on the horse ranch. It's Moonlit Horse Sanctuary, so they take in horses that have been abused and they get them healthy and socialized again. They have a bunkhouse for ranch hands," Asher answered.

"I'll be going to Fort Moore in Georgia

and staying on base there for Basic training. Afterward, I might be stationed there or moved to another base. I won't know until after Basic is completed."

I wasn't too worried about Greyson finding a place to live. The military always had dorms or places for their soldiers to live in every town they were in. It was Asher who was my main concern, as usual, but he'd found a ranch that had a bunkhouse so he wouldn't have to worry about finding a place or even paying rent. All he had to do was pay for his food, cell phone, and gas for his truck. At least they were both going to be fine and taken care of.

"All right, good. I have to get going so I don't miss my flight. I want you both to text me every day and let me know when you will be leaving. I mean it, no more secrets, no matter what."

"We promise," Asher said on their behalf, both of them dragging me in for a backslapping hug.

I would have loved to be home to see them off, but I couldn't put this training course off. If I wanted to be a Smokejumper, I had to take this course and with them now being legal adults, I didn't have to worry about leaving them alone for a month. I'd waited a long time for this opportunity and I wasn't about to blow it.

This was my chance, my time, to be my own adult, my own person without obligations or responsibilities to other people. It was different and it was going to take some getting used to, but it was something that I had to do. It was something all three of us had to do. We had been living for each other for so long and now it was our time to be our own individuals and live our lives.

I just hoped it wouldn't be too terrible of an adjustment period for the three of us. Only time would tell. I prayed they got everything they wanted out of life, because they deserved it and I couldn't be more proud of them.

CHAPTER FOUR

Xavier

I HATED THE first day of a new training class. The students were always filled with so much joy and excitement that it was like trying to teach a group of thirty puppies how to sit and shut up. Most of them were in their mid-twenties and older, all of which were younger than mid-thirties. The simple fact was there was a point where a body couldn't handle the physical requirements of being a Smokejumper. That and normally it took a young buck to be stupid enough to do this job. I, of course, was the exception, but I came from a war zone, so this was nothing to me.

I could see they were all feeling pumped and ready for this, but I also knew that would quickly change. The first few days were the honeymoon period. Where they all thought it was easy and they were going to graduate and get their certificate. Normally, on day five was when reality would hit them and they would feel how exhausted and sore their bodies were. They would learn that they couldn't be a complete idiot if they were going to be able to understand all of the weather graphs and be able to predict how a fire would move. There was a lot more book smarts to it than people expected. They figured they would ride on a chopper, repel down, and then fight a fire, but that simplicity of it all was how you got yourself and others killed. You had to be able to understand the weather side of things to properly save people's lives.

"What do you think?" Jackson came up beside me and asked.

He was one of the guys that I worked with often. I wasn't really based out of a firehouse because what I did required me to be up in the air for the most part. Jackson did search and rescue, so whenever someone was lost in the woods or hurt, he went in to save 'em. He was talented at what he did and he was double certified for search and rescue and also medical. If that wasn't enough, he had a beautiful golden retriever that would go with him on his searches.

"I think they're all idiots," I said with zero humor in my voice.

I did like Jackson. He was one of the good ones to be around. He was older like I was, and still going strong. You would never know he was forty-five, he looked ten years younger, and he acted like a horny twenty year old. Jackson was the guy that your parents warned you to stay away from. He was the guy you didn't bring home to your parents, because he would never be there two weekends later. He was the type of guy that I would never want Dexter to be with, not that Dexter was gay, but my point still stands.

"There's those people skills again," Jackson said, flashing a smirk before he continued. "Some of them look delicious."

"There's those people skills," I countered with my own smirk that caused Jackson to laugh.

That was one of the nice things about Jackson, he didn't try to change me or judge me. He understood that I was damaged and he accepted who I was. Some of the others were always trying to get me to go out or to see someone. They wanted me to find a hobby and all that bullshit. Jackson didn't, he was just there and I really appreciated it. That was probably why we were good friends.

He was actually the only person that I would call a friend. It helped that his father had been in service and he had an older brother that was in service. Both were killed in action, but he understood the toll the job took on people. So he never gave me shit or looked at me with pity when I was drinking. He never tried to drag me out during the day to busy places. He was perfectly happy to hang out at his place or go to one of the smaller gay bars.

"Come on, you have to admit that some of them are looking very sexy."

"How many times do we have to have this conversation? You aren't supposed to sleep with any of the cadets."

"It's not my fault there's always one gay guy or bi-curious guy in the group. I bet you there's at least one here right now."

"Weren't you interested in that other guy? The one you met at the strip club."

Jackson didn't date in the traditional sense. He tended to have the guys he was with believing that they were special and could make him change. That they were the ones that would change his ways and make him fall in love. He didn't advise them against that belief. He would be sleeping with them, but also sleeping with others. He usually had a few guys on the go at the same time, most of which didn't know about the others. He was a dog, a dirty down dog, but he had his reasons, I'm sure. We'd never talked about it, but I was certain there was something in his history that made him that way. I respected him enough to not press, just like he had never pressed me for more answers.

"I was and we were hooking up for a few months before he found out that I was also seeing three other guys," he said with a small shrug.

"How did he find out? You're normally

more careful than that."

"He's got a younger brother that walked in on me with one of my other honeys at the club. He told Devon and apparently Devon felt like we were exclusive and he wasn't looking for an open relationship."

"I'm surprised you weren't trying to get with the younger brother. You always like them young and dumb."

"He's eighteen, but he's not dumb, and he's not your typical eighteen year old, at least according to Devon. He's got a good head on his shoulders and doesn't like meaningless sex. He's like a seventy-year-old man trapped in an eighteen year old's body."

"The horror of responsible sexual activity," I said sarcastically. The kid sounded smart and like he knew what he wanted out of life and he wasn't letting anything get in his way.

"It's the worst thing in the world. But enough about my very active sex life, we have to get started before the natives get restless."

I gave a slight hum in agreement before we both made our way toward the front of the classroom. Everyone was in different groups and talking, they didn't even notice us at the front ready to go.

"That's enough! Take your seats!" I called out.

"These poor cadets have no idea what they are in for," Jackson mumbled next to me and I knew he meant about my attitude. I wasn't the friendliest teacher, but I was the one that would give them the best chance at living.

All of the cadets turned their attention

to me and I could see it registering in their mind that it was time to get started. They all made their way to their seats and I could see they all had a small notebook and a pen with them. They really were expecting this to be more hands-on and it would be, eventually, but there were a lot of classroom hours and an exam as well.

"My name is Xavier Cruz, I will be one of your main instructors for this course. I will also be your pilot. This is my colleague, Jackson Hall. You will see him for the medical side of things for the course. He is one of the best search and rescue firefighters in the country. When they have someone they can't find, they call for Jackson. He's been all over the country searching for people who have gone missing in complex forestry locations. This course is a month long, six days a week. In order to qualify for your certificate, you must score eighty percent or higher on your final written and practical exam. Anything under, even by one decimal point, and you will not receive your certificate. Any questions so far?"

I was hoping not. I hadn't gotten into anything technical so there shouldn't be any questions right now. Thankfully no one raised their hand.

"Today, I will be taking you up in groups so you can see the area that this course will be about. You will get to have aerial views in class, but seeing it in person helps you to visualize the area. Those who are not up in the air with me, will be meeting with the head doctor to go over your medical history. We need to know everything so there are no surprises that come up. When every group has had a turn, we will then be doing class work for the next week."

"A week?" One of the cadets said.

I had no idea who he was. It wasn't like they were wearing nametags. I nodded and moved on.

"Half of this course is done in the field and the other half is done in a classroom. Something you all should know if you actually read the course program before you applied to be here. You have to be able to read weather maps, understand wind speeds, wind structures, and how it can all change based on the weather forecast that is moving in. All of that helps you accurately predict the path of the fire. Being able to predict how the fire is going to move will allow you to evacuate the cities that are in the destruction path.

It also allows you to try and contain the fire to prevent it from spreading further. Every firefighter, whether on the ground or in the air, has to be able to read the fire. You can't rely on someone else to be able to do it because you could be separated and your very life depends on it. If you are not going to take this seriously, then leave. Do not waste our time."

That was something I was not going to tolerate. I didn't have a problem teaching those who were willing. You didn't have to be the smartest person in the world; I just needed you to try. If they weren't going to try, then they could get the hell out of here and make room for the people that were committed to being here and learning.

"This isn't going to be easy for you. We

know that learning a new skill in the classroom can be very difficult for people. We have no problem taking the time and working through it with you. But we're not going to put that time in if you aren't committed to learning. If you thought this was going to be you repelling out of a chopper for the next four weeks, you were wrong. Just like you have to be able to read a fire in a building, you have to be able to read a fire in the forest. But like I said, we will help you as long as you are willing to learn," Jackson added.

I could see a mixture of reactions within the group. Some were annoyed that they would have to be stuck in a classroom. They completely thought this was going to be fully hands-on. Others were content to learn what they had to so they could get through this course.

However, a couple looked excited for it all.

They were excited to learn a new skill and it was those that I was looking forward to teaching. It was refreshing and more enjoyable to teach someone who wanted to learn. Someone who literally loved to learn. I had come across a few firefighters who just wanted to learn new skills so they could help more people. It made for a great learning experience and I was hoping the ones who wanted to learn made it through the course.

"All right, I need you four right there for the first flight up." I pointed at the four in the first row. "The rest of you will be meeting with our Doc one at a time. When you are not with the doc, we have a workbook for you to start going over. It covers basic information that you most likely learned in the Fire Academy, but you don't utilize it every day on the job. It's important to remember the basics so we can build up on it. Jackson will be here to answer any questions that you have."

They were getting busy work today, but we really did need to make sure they knew the basics so we could build on them. If they didn't remember all of the basics we had to cover that real quick, otherwise they were going to be confused down the road.

"Have fun," Jackson said with a short wave to me before I headed off and gave a nod to the four guys who would be coming with me on the first trip. It was going to be a long ass day for me and all I could do was hope that I didn't snap at any of their questions. I was still hung over from last night so I just needed this to go smoothly today.

CHAPTER FIVE

Gage

WELL, TODAY HADN'T gone like I thought it would. When I first got here, I was excited and filled with so much energy at the prospect of learning a new skill. I'd always loved to learn something useful.

I didn't care too much about school when I was younger, because I had to focus on taking care of everyone. School growing up took a backseat in my life, a very far backseat, like the nosebleed section. Being in the Fire Academy allowed me to learn all these different skills and to be able to utilize them in real life. I loved every minute of it and I was hoping that this would be similar.

I had read the course outline before I decided to take the course. I didn't just jump in like some of the others had based on the name alone. I wanted to make sure it was what I thought it was going to be and it was, but also with a lot more technical aspects than I had initially expected.

I would be lying if I didn't say I wasn't a little bit worried about the class work. It wasn't that I wasn't smart, I was, but I was also a lot like Asher in that sense. I didn't have the fancy math or science classes that Greyson took, but only because I had to take what I could just barely get away with in high school. I honestly didn't know if I would be able to understand half of the course work, but I was willing to do everything in my power to learn it.

Meeting with the doctor hadn't been a big deal. I had always been a healthy guy. I didn't have any previous surgeries or any bad breaks. I'd only broken a couple of fingers and my wrist once since being on the job.

I took my job seriously, especially because I had two kids at home who were counting on me to come back alive and in one piece. I was always anal about safety and making sure that I was aware of my surroundings to reduce the risk of injuries or death. It had still been a long process though, to cover everything from my birth practically until now.

I hadn't been picked for a group yet, so my group was last and I was hoping the previous group hadn't gotten back yet. I didn't know what would happen if I missed my chance to go up there today. It was getting a bit later in the afternoon, almost five o'clock, and I wasn't certain how long Xavier would be flying with it being closer to winter and it getting darker out earlier.

The second I walked back into the classroom my heart sank. The other three that I was to be going up with weren't there. I had missed them. I saw the other teacher, Jackson, coming toward me and I hoped he wasn't going to tell me to just go to the dorms for the night.

"Hey, he took them up about thirty

minutes ago. He didn't know how long you would be so he is flying them around and then he will take you up for a solo flight. Afterward, you can head back to the dorms and grab some food and rest up for tomorrow."

"Thanks. I'm assuming that is where everyone else is."

"Yeah, they left thirty minutes ago. They all seemed very thankful to be leaving. I guess we don't have any bookworms in the group," he said, flashing me an easy smile.

I had noticed that Jackson seemed to be the friendlier instructor. I didn't know if Xavier was really that unfriendly or if he was just serious. I had known a few instructors in the Fire Academy who were hardasses in the classroom, but once you got outside of it they were the life of the party and all smiles. It just depended on how they taught. Some found it easier to be friendly the whole time and others found it was better to keep the two lives separate.

There was also the chance that Xavier was like that all the time, in which case, he would be terrible to go for a beer with. Only time would tell. The good news was, if he was an asshole all the time I only had to deal with him for the next thirty days and then I would never have to see him again. Most likely, anyway. The odds of him being my chopper pilot going into a fire were pretty slim. Even if it did happen, I would only have to see him in small doses.

I made my way over to my seat and continued on with the booklet. I knew most of the guys weren't taking it very seriously. To them the basics were already instilled in their minds and they didn't need the refresher. I got it, we were all Alpha males, practically. To me though, I wanted to make sure there weren't any areas that I had forgotten about or maybe I wasn't that good at something. If there were areas that I needed improvement on, I wanted to know before things in the classroom got complicated. Besides, working on it was better than staring at the walls waiting for the chopper to land. I was relieved though, to know that most of the basics had stuck with me and maybe that was because I wasn't too many years out of the academy. It had only been seven for me, compared to seventeen for some of the guys here.

It was a good hour later when I heard

the thumping of the chopper propellers coming down. It was getting pretty dark out now and I was starting to question if I was going up tonight or not. I knew Xavier would have flown at night, you can't exactly only fight a forest fire during the day; however, that was when he had to and technically he didn't have to take me up tonight. I was hoping we would be, but at the same time I could understand why we wouldn't go. It certainly would be easier to go during daylight hours so I could see the ground and different land markings. I couldn't exactly do that at night.

I watched as the guys came in and I could see they were excited and talking about what they had experienced. I wished I could have gone up with them, because something was telling me that going up one-on-one with Xavier wasn't going to leave me feeling that excited.

I watched as Xavier walked in and he looked the opposite of the others. He looked very annoyed and just done with life. I guess I couldn't blame him. He didn't seem like the type who would enjoy teaching others or being trapped in a tin can ten thousand feet in the air with no escape. It wasn't making me feel good about my turn with him.

He went over to Jackson first, not even looking in my direction, and I could see them talking but I couldn't hear them. The look on Xavier's face didn't change, but I wasn't certain if that was a good thing or not. After a minute, Jackson gave a nod and headed out before Xavier finally turned his attention to me. I could have sworn he grew more annoyed that I was still here.

"Let's go," he ordered before he headed out the door, not even checking to see if I was following him. I wanted to be annoyed, but he was at least taking me up so I wasn't going to push my luck.

I grabbed my jacket before I followed him out. By the time I got there, he was already in the pilot seat. I quickly jumped into the passenger side and put the headphones on so I could hear him. He didn't speak though, not a single word, as he got the blades spinning and took us into the sky.

I suddenly felt like I was sitting outside the Principal's office waiting to find out how much shit I was going to be in. A situation that had happened a good dozen times in my life in both grade school and high school. It was never because I had bullied someone or gotten into a fight, it was always about my school work or missed days. Apparently, their sympathy for my sick and dying mother could only go so far. Not that I expected it to work for me the whole time, but it would have been nice for it to last a bit longer.

"How do you see the land markings at night?" I asked, breaking the silence between us. I wished I could say the silence was comfortable. It was more like animosity and I had no idea why. It wasn't like I had done something to him.

"There is a light on the bottom of the chopper that will allow you to see. When there is a forest fire, it lights up the sky and makes it easy to see. If the smoke gets too thick, every chopper's lights are able to penetrate the fog."

I knew the lights on the chopper were

powerful, but I also knew it wasn't as easy as Xavier was making it sound. I knew the smoke from a fire could choke up the engine and cause the whirlybird to go down too. That was the deadly balancing game that every pilot had to face every single time they went up in the air. If they stayed too long, they risked the chopper going down and hurting or killing everyone inside. On the other side of the coin though, if they stopped too soon, then the fire spread and they risked the people who were trapped inside dying. A pilot really had to know their helicopter and how its engine was feeling. It wasn't easy and I had serious respect for every pilot, because it wasn't something I would be able to handle. That was too much stress and I would be a ball of anxiety before I even got the thing off the ground.

I'd stick to fighting fires.

"And I'm going to be able to see this during the day too, right?"

"Assuming you make it that far."

Wow.

I knew he didn't know me and he had no reason to believe that I would be able to get through this course, but come on. He didn't even know me. I don't even think he knew my name. He could have at least a little bit of faith in me. I was a firefighter, had been for seven years, so I obviously knew what I was doing to still be alive. I wasn't a novice, but it felt like I was this annoying teenager Xavier had to deal with. Before I could even comment there was a bang right before the chopper shook and I knew that wasn't normal.

"What was that?" I instantly asked, but Xavier didn't say anything. I wanted to be annoyed, but I was more worried about the look of confusion and worry that overtook his face. For a man who seemed to have one hell of a poker face, his really sucked right now.

Another bang echoed off of the metal walls of the chopper. Whatever hit the chopper was stronger this time, because it wasn't even a second later when we were in a full tailspin.

"Fuck!" Xavier yelled as he fought to get the helicopter to stop spinning and level us out again. "Hold on, we're going down."

"What?" I grabbed onto the metal bar attached to the door, but I knew it wasn't going to be doing much if we were going to crash. This was insane. My first time in a chopper and we were going to crash.

Fuck my life.

Xavier didn't elaborate, but I didn't think he would. He was too busy trying to level out the chopper and, hopefully, land us down smoothly. I knew it wasn't going to happen though. We were over ten thousand feet and whatever hit us, they got our tail, which is what Xavier needed to keep the chopper leveled out.

I kept my gaze on him. I was too terrified to look out any of the windows to see the trees and ground getting closer. So I kept my eyes glued on him, on his face and his arms, as his bicep muscles bulked out from the sheer strength he had to use to try and keep the chopper leveled out so he could attempt to land us. It wasn't going to be a smooth landing, even though the main propellers were working. Without the tail there was nothing to keep us balanced while in the air. The chopper would be useless to get us back to the training facility.

My body jerked around as we finally hit the thick trees and we both thrashed around as we rolled and free fell down the rest of the drop until we finally crashed into the hard ground.

My head was pounding. It had smacked against the passenger door window and I could have sworn there was blood going down the right side of my face. We landed on the side, my side, and I could feel the ache in my head, but also my entire right side as it smashed into the door. I could see the front windshield was a mess of spiderweb cracks and I could have sworn I smelled smoke.

I managed to turn my head to look at Xavier and I was relieved to see that he was awake. He was hanging above me, thanks to his seatbelt. I knew we couldn't stay here though. If I could smell smoke that meant the chopper was smoking and there was a good chance it would go up in flames. I really didn't want to be here if that should happen.

I moved my left hand up and hit the middle clip for the seatbelt and released the multiple parts that clicked together. I was already on the ground, but my body still jerked forward slightly. I pushed myself up to my knees as I spoke.

"Xavier, we gotta get out of here. Can you unclick yourself?"

"Yeah, once you move out of the way I can drop down. Kick out the windshield and crawl out."

I didn't need to be told twice.

I climbed down to the front of my seat and kicked at the windshield. Even though it was already cracked all to hell, it was still difficult to get it to detach from the frame of the chopper. I didn't have much room to pull my legs back to give myself some real power behind each kick. After a good five times, I was able to get it off and I crawled out.

I immediately looked back at the chopper to see if I could pinpoint where the smoke was coming from. It was coming from the tail and the engine of the chopper. There were no flames yet and I hoped that maybe we got lucky and nothing explosive was compromised from the crash.

A bang sounded and I turned to see Xavier had gotten out of his seat and landed in a crouch just in front of the passenger seat. He didn't come out right away though, but went into the back of the chopper looking for something.

I hoped it was a radio or flashlights. It was dark as shit out here and I knew it was going to be getting worse before the sun started to rise. Just like I knew it was only going to be getting colder out. This was supposed to be a fun and easy trip around a designated area and now we were stranded in the forest with next to no supplies. This was not how I saw this course going.

Not even fucking close.

CHAPTER SIX

Xavier

FUCKING SHIT.

All I had to do was take one more trip around the training area, just one fucking more, and then I could go home and get drunk in peace. Just a quick fly around the training area and then back to base. Simple, but no. Nope, I couldn't possibly be that lucky, not me. No, instead we got shot down by some fucking rebel survivalists that are more paranoid then a dozen schizophrenics in a nut house.

I didn't even need to think about who could have shot at us. We had been getting threatening letters for months now from the extremists who seem to believe we are some Government agency spying on them. They had threatened to shoot at us before, but we, *I,* never took it seriously because any idiot could see that the chopper was bright orange with the fire department insignia on it. Clearly we were not spies or the Feds looking to invade their encampment.

Apparently, they didn't fucking care though.

I guess it was a good thing that I only had the one cadet with me, whatever his name was, and not a full group. The last thing I wanted to deal with was four cadets all shaking in their boots because we crashed. This wasn't my first crash. It was the first since I had left the military, sure, but at least when I crashed overseas there were gunfights afterward. I wasn't going to have to worry about that here. The biggest threat to us was getting hypothermia out here.

I searched the back of the chopper for what little supplies it had. It wasn't really stocked for a trip through the woods. I didn't even have blankets because this wasn't a rescue mission, it was just a quick tour. I grabbed the two flashlights and the radio that I had. I also went to grab for the radios, but they were all smashed from the trip down to the ground.

Fuck.

It looked like we were walking back whether we wanted to or not. I knew the area, but it was still going to be a couple of days before we made it back. At least come morning when we both didn't show up Jackson would know something was wrong. But without any flares and no way of getting word about our location, it was going to take Jackson some time to find the chopper. Hopefully, the black box was still intact and he would be able to pull up the GPS.

I knew it would make the most sense to hide out here and wait for the rescue chopper to show up. With some luck, we would be able to find a place that would block some of the cold wind and it would keep us warmer until the sun came up. The last thing I wanted to be doing right now was wandering through the fucking woods, and hopefully the universe would give us this break.

I headed back out and turned the flashlights on. I pointed them in the direction of where I thought the cadet was and I was pleased to see he was at least standing. He had blood trickling down the side of his face though, and my initial concern was a potential concussion. If he was concussed, it would make the night a hell of a lot longer. I went over to him and held out the other flashlight for him before I turned my attention to his head.

"Does it hurt?"

"I'm fine," he said, but I wasn't in the mood for his macho bullshit.

"I'm trying to determine if you have a concussion. Answer the questions."

I knew I was snapping at him. I knew this wasn't his fault. He missed his turn with his group because he was with the Doc. It wasn't his fault we were out later than I wanted to be. It wasn't his fault that we got shot down by rednecks. Still, he was the only one here and my anger didn't care about any rational thoughts.

"It's tender, but I'm not dizzy or nauseous. And your obnoxious flashlight in my eyes doesn't make it hurt any worse. Now, get your hands off of me and tell me what the fuck just happened."

He had every right to be just as angry as I was and yet hearing it directed toward me only fueled my own anger. We were both victims of circumstances, but my mind refused to remember that every time he opened his mouth. I had to get a grip on my emotions. I was the senior man in charge here and I needed to take control with a rational mind.

"Survival extremists within the area have been sending threatening letters to the Station about the choppers. They seem to believe we are the Government and spying on their land. They have threatened to shoot the choppers out of the sky, but we didn't think they would actually do it. Our choppers don't exactly blend in and scream Federal Agents."

"Great. Fucking great. Radio?" he asked as he started to pace around. I was getting the feeling he wasn't used to just standing still for very long. Because that would make my night even more complete; an ADHD cadet in the fucking woods.

I was getting too old for this shit.

"Broke on the crash down. We don't have much. I was only supposed to take everyone around the training area. Wasn't exactly planning on a midnight stroll. The black box is most likely still intact. Our best bet is to find a place to hunker down for the night. Once we're not there in the morning Jackson will know something went wrong and pull up the GPS on the helo. He'll come out and we will be back at the station before lunch."

This wasn't going to be up for debate, we were going to hide out and just wait. Thankfully he gave me a nod and I knew we were at least in agreement.

I stood where I was and turned in a circle as I moved the light around the area. I knew what it looked like from above, but I hadn't seen this place on the ground. It looked different when it wasn't from ten thousand feet.

I didn't want to go too far away from the crash site. Jackson would come to this area first and with the trees being so thick it was going to be harder for him to see us from the sky. There wasn't a place for him to land so we would have to be repelled up to the chopper. We had to be close by and in some type of clearing, even a small one so we could be spotted. All of that was not easy when it was so fucking dark out though.

"What about there?" the cadet asked and I went and looked at where he was pointing his flashlight. It was a set of large boulders, but the way they were positioned it created a man made cave in a sense. It would be a tight fit, but we would be able to manage and it would help to prevent the wind hitting us from three sides. It was roughly five hundred feet from the chopper, close enough that we would be able to hear Jackson come morning.

"That'll work," I said, before I started to walk over there. I could hear him following behind me and I was glad that I didn't hear him stumbling.

The second I was at the little cave, I went in first and I was not surprised to see that it wasn't all that deep. We would just fit and it was going to be tight, but it would work for the night. This wasn't the first time I had to sleep rough or not sleep at all. I didn't know about him though, and I really hoped he wasn't the bitching type. The last thing I wanted to deal with was listening to someone whine all night about being cold or the hard ground.

I sat down on the ground with my back against the cold rock. The cadet sat across from me on the other rock wall and he had his knees up to his chest. There was only enough space in the cave for us to sit down with our legs kept close to our body. I was sitting with my legs crossed; I was too big to sit with my legs up against my chest. I was actually surprised that he could because he wasn't much smaller than I was.

He kept his eyes locked on the outside of our little cave and he didn't seem to be in the mood to talk, something I was relieved about because I wasn't in the mood to make small talk all night. I had to admit though, now that I was getting the chance to just sit and look at him, he was good looking. Even with the shadows from the flashlight playing across his face, he was attractive. He wasn't man-pretty like Jackson liked, but he was handsome, rugged, the type of guy that I found attractive. Though, they weren't normally his size. I tended to go for smaller guys, the type where I knew they were a bottom. If this cadet was gay, I wouldn't even know if he was a top or bottom.

Our pleasurable silence came to an end when the cadet decided to open his very sexy mouth and ruin it.

"Will the black box work if the chopper blows up?"

"Yeah, it's designed to handle fires and being submerged in water."

It was a reasonable question so I had no problem answering it. The black box was our only hope of being found; it was logical that he would be concerned about it. I was just hoping that the smoke was nothing more than the engine being overheated and not the sign of something seriously wrong with it. The chopper itself was a write off, there was no fixing it, but the last thing I wanted to worry about was it blowing up and accidentally starting a forest fire. That wasn't the hands-on experience I was looking to offer for this course.

"You got any kids, a wife?" he asked next.

"We don't have to talk," I instantly said. The last thing I wanted to do was make small talk with this guy for the next twelve hours.

"You want to sit here in the dark and cold all night long and not say a single word?" he countered as he looked over at me. I could tell he wasn't too happy with that idea, but it sounded perfect to me.

"You want to share your darkest secrets around the campfire?" I countered sarcastically. Maybe if he was annoyed enough he would shut the hell up.

"There's no campfire and I wouldn't consider having children or a wife being a dark secret. Unless it's actually a husband and you are too ashamed to admit that you like cock over pussy," he countered, flashing me a cocky smirk.

I wanted to punch it off his face.

It was none of his business if I was gay or straight. It was none of his business if I had kids or not. My life was none of his business, just like his life wasn't any of mine. We were not friends. We were not colleagues. I was his instructor and he was my cadet. It was a professional, barely, relationship and that was all it would ever be.

"I'm your instructor, your superior, it would be best that you remember that when you speak to me. I can send you right back to whatever State you came from for insubordination and being disrespectful to the chain of command. Do you understand me, Cadet?"

Maybe that was harsh, but he needed to learn his place. He needed to learn that I was not his friend, nor did I want to be. I had done the whole friends thing. It always ended with me having to bury them and I wasn't about to bury another friend, another person I cared about. It was better to be alone. If I got lonely, fuck, that's what whiskey was for.

"Yes, Sir." His tone was borderline disgusted and I could tell he wasn't happy with me.

In my opinion, there were three types of people in the world. The type who always gave someone respect because they were their superior and they respected the chain of command without question. The second type never gave the other respect regardless of their rank, because they were little assholes and their mommy and daddy didn't teach them about respect. The third type though, they were the ones that had no problem giving respect, but you had to earn it. This cadet was either the second or third type and my gut was leading me toward the second type. We were never going to get along and I highly doubted that he would make it through this course. If he couldn't respect me, then he was never getting in my chopper again.

He turned his attention back out toward the helicopter and I was glad that he was keeping his mouth shut this time. I'd had some pretty long and horrible nights in my life, but I was getting the feeling that this night was going to be right up there with them.

CHAPTER SEVEN

Gage

WHAT AN ASSHOLE. If he wants to sit here all night and not say anything, fine. Two can play that game. I once played the silent game with the twins for four days and won. A night in a makeshift cave, shit this was nothing.

A quick glance over in his direction and I saw that he had his eyes closed. I didn't know if he was asleep or just looking to rest his eyes. I honestly didn't care which option it was, it was better than him staring at me. Not going to lie though, there was a large part of me that wanted to just start singing the most annoying song I could think of.

Was it childish?

Absolutely.

Did he deserve it?

Fucking yes, he did.

Apparently, Xavier was the type of leader who demanded respect without earning a shred of it. I knew there needed to be some level of respect at first. He was my superior and I knew that meant I had to respect him; however, I also knew that full respect was not freely given. He had to earn it. He had to show me that I could give him that respect, that he was worthy of it and so far, he hadn't shown me he deserved that level of respect from me.

I knew most people would have freely given it, but that wasn't who I was. That wasn't something I was capable of doing. I had been screwed over too many times to trust blindly, to give full respect blindly. It might seem silly to others, but not to me.

A small flicker of light caught my eye and I turned my full attention into the darkness within the woods. I knew we weren't around any roads, so it wouldn't have been the headlights of a passing vehicle. I knew it was possible that my mind was playing tricks on me, but I could have sworn I saw a light. Another flicker behind the trees proved me right. Someone was out there.

Part of me wanted to be happy, excited, that someone was out there.

Someone who might have seen the crash or was out for an evening stroll. People camped in these woods so it wouldn't be that far of a stretch to think they heard or saw the crash. They also could have been a camper looking to take a leak. They might have a radio or a phone that had a signal that we could use to call Jackson and get out of here before sunrise.

"Hey," I said as I lightly hit Xavier's calf.

"What?" Xavier responded and I could see that he didn't even bother with opening his eyes.

"Someone's out there."

That seemed to get his attention. His eyes snapped open and he instantly looked out of our little cave. I wasn't certain what I expected his reaction to be, but I was surprised to see that he appeared to be more worried than anything else.

This was a good thing, right?

We could get out of here tonight and sleep in an actual bed.

More lights started to appear and now I was starting to worry, because there shouldn't be a dozen people in the woods. It was the end of fall; it would be too cold for a large group to go camping. One or two, sure. People camped in the winter, but they were dedicated campers and they had the proper equipment they needed to survive the weather. A dozen people didn't just decide to go on a camping trip together in this weather. We could hear voices, but I couldn't hear everything they were saying. It was clear though they were looking for the chopper.

The sound of movement next to me

made me turn my head slightly to see that Xavier had moved and he spoke softly into my ear. "It's the extremists. They think we were Feds and they want to hold us hostage, get news coverage. We have to move. Don't turn the flashlight on and stay close to me."

Holy fuck.

As if this night hadn't been bad enough, now we were going to have to play hide and seek with the gun-toting extremists.

Xavier moved before me and he stepped over me before he grabbed my hand and pulled me. I just managed to get up without falling over and being dragged by him.

I knew we had to be quiet; we couldn't risk them overhearing us. What was difficult though, was walking through the woods without the use of the flashlights. I couldn't see anything and it was very difficult to not trip on any of the tree roots that were sticking up. We were trying to be quiet, but that wasn't all that simple when every step we took made a crunching sound of dry leaves and twigs under our feet.

We didn't even make it fifteen feet when a light hit us followed by a loud male voice. "There they are!"

I didn't know what I had been expecting to happen next, but the sound of a bullet hitting a tree by our head was not one of them. Before I could even process what was happening Xavier was pulling me as he started to take off at a run. I had no choice but to run with him or risk getting my arm pulled out of the socket.

I ran as fast as I could, trying to keep up with him. I wanted to pull my hand out of his, but not only did he have a death grip on it, but I also had no idea where we were going. Xavier knew the area, even if it was from the sky, he knew the area better than me and if we separated right now, there was a high risk that I wouldn't be able to keep up with him and then we would really be separated and the last thing I wanted to do was be lost in the woods alone with the rednecks.

I had no idea how long we kept running for. All I knew was that my lungs were burning and my legs felt like jell-o, but we kept going. The gunfire had stopped at least. I suspected that the rednecks were unable to track us right now with it being dark, but I highly doubted they were going to pack up and go back home. They thought we were Feds and they wanted a show. They wanted to parade us out front of cameras to prove their point to the world. We were too valuable to them and their beliefs to just let us go.

And because this night hadn't fucking sucked enough, it had started to pour rain hours ago. We were both soaking wet, exhausted, and I was starving. Not to mention we both were filthy from slipping in the mud. We needed a break. We needed a chance to catch our breaths. We needed a chance to get out of this rain.

"Xavier, stop," I managed to get out. Fuck, even talking was taking me a minute.

To my utmost pleasure, he did stop. He was breathing just as heavily as I was and I knew he wouldn't be able to go much longer, much like myself. It didn't matter that we were both fit and weren't ones to shy away from cardio day, this was a lot of running on rough and uneven terrain and it was fucking pouring out. Plus, it was so dark we couldn't see our own hand in front of our face. This was far from an ideal environment, but we had made it work. Now we needed to find a place to wait out the storm, something I was hoping the extremists were doing.

"We have to find a place to bunker down. We can't keep going, not like this."

I really hoped he wasn't going to disagree and tell me to suck it up, that we had to keep moving. I honestly didn't think I could keep moving. My whole body was sore and my legs were seconds away from giving out. It was going to be a miracle for me to keep moving while we looked for a place that we could hide out in.

"I know. If I'm right on our location, there is a cave about ten minutes just north of here. We should be far enough away from them to hide out for the rest of the night," he said with a heavy breath and I could hear him gasping for air in his overexerted lungs.

"Okay," I managed to get out, grateful that he at least agreed easily. What I wanted to say was *thank fucking god*, but I didn't want him to know just how much I was struggling.

I kept my hand in his as we started to lightly jog this time. It wasn't any better than running, but it would at least get us to the cave faster and then we could rest. It was not lost on me that going from running to just nothing wasn't good on your body. It would cause our muscles to spasm and tighten up. Something as simple as walking tomorrow would be hilariously painful. My mind couldn't help but conjure up the image of the Tin Man without his oilcan. It was really funny when I put Xavier's face on that mental image. I guess the good thing was that we were too exhausted and out of breath to even speak to each other.

By the time we made it to the cave, I felt like I was going to pass out. It took every last ounce of energy that I had to make it inside the cave. This time it was a legitimate cave and there was enough room for both of us to stand and move around. I was worried about bears, but apparently Xavier wasn't.

"How do we know if we're alone in

here?" I couldn't help but ask.

"The migration patterns don't have any bears in this area right now. A few more weeks and there will be. We have to get out of our clothes."

"What?" My sluggish mind couldn't seem to follow that train of thought.

Why would we be getting naked?

"Hypothermia. We have to get out of our wet clothes and use each other's body heat to get warm. Strip, Cadet," he said with a bit of an edge to his voice that I didn't particularly appreciate, especially given he wanted me to get naked for him.

"Gage," I said as I tried to get my brain to tell my hands to move.

"What?" It was his turn to be confused and I couldn't help but smirk.

How do you like it?

"My name isn't Cadet, it's Gage. And

considering you want me to get naked for you, the least you could do is bother to remember my name."

He was right, we had to use each other's body heat but that didn't mean I was going to make it easier on this asshole.

"Fine, take your clothes off, *Gage*," he said with a snippy attitude.

I would let that go, for now.

I got my coat off and was about to get my shirt off when I heard him let out a groan. It wasn't a sound of discomfort, but pain. I wished I could see him better, but it was too dark to see anything.

"Where are you hurt?" I really hoped he wasn't going to pull some macho bullshit and tell me he was fine. I was not in the mood to play that game.

"I'm fi—" Before he even had a chance

to finish that bullshit statement, I cut him off.

"I swear to fucking god if you tell me you are fine I am going to punch you. And considering it's dark, I have no idea where that punch will land. At the rate our luck is going, I'll end up punching you in the nuts. So unless you would like to play Russian roulette on your balls, give me a goddamn fucking honest answer. It's been too long of a night for this shit."

Now, I acknowledge that I could have been a bit nicer about it. But in my defense, this had been the longest night of my life and I didn't even think it was half over. He was not my superior right now. He was some guy that I just met and got stranded in the woods with. That's all we were, just a couple of guys trying not to get our heads blown off by some fucking radicals with riffles. Like we were in a Steven King novel. It wouldn't surprise me if there was a bear in this cave with us, because that is how my luck had been going since I left Baton Rouge. So yes, I could have been nicer, but at the same time I didn't have any fucks left to give tonight. Completely sold out until I got a hot shower, a double bacon cheeseburger, and about eight hours of sleep in a warm and soft bed.

He let out a sigh, a fucking sigh, like I was the impatient child on a road trip asking if we were there yet, before he spoke. "A bullet grazed my right bicep. I will be fine."

Right, because getting grazed by a bullet was a completely natural thing.

Oh, Jesus fuck.

Okay, medically getting grazed isn't

really a big deal. A few stitches and the wound would heal itself, but we had been running and falling down in mud, so chances were that the graze on his arm was now a mess of blood and mud.

"We need to clean it out before it gets infected. We can use the rain to wash it out, but we'll have to turn on one of the flashlights for a minute or two." He wasn't going to like that idea.

"Absolutely not."

Yup, called it.

Couldn't actually agree on one thing, that would make this way too easy and who wanted an easy life?

Sigh.

"I can cover it with my hand to reduce the brightness, but we have to use the light long enough for you to clean that wound. The last thing we need is you getting an infection. If those guys show up, we both have to be able to fight and run. Two things that can't happen if you are fighting off an infection."

I just needed him to agree with me on this. I didn't want to argue about this for very long, but I couldn't let it go because the threat was still real out there.

"All right," he growled. "Cover the light with both of your hands. We can go to the entrance of the cave and I can wash it out." He'd caved and I was so fucking thankful for it.

"Okay," I said, knowing he wouldn't be able to see me nod.

We both wandered over to the entrance of the cave. I placed the end of the flashlight under my armpit and turned it on before I cupped my hands around the outside of the light. It made it dimmer, but bright enough that we would be able to see the injury. It looked deep to me and my gut said he needed stitches. We would have to try and keep it as clean as possible until we got back to the station.

Xavier had already pulled his shirt off and he quickly used the rainwater to wash the blood and mud from his cut. It was down and dirty, but that was all we really had right now. With it cleaned, I turned the light back off and we made our way back into the cave and further away from the wind and rain.

We both removed our clothing and I felt like an idiot standing there naked, not really sure what I was supposed to do. If I had been with a guy that I knew was gay, I wouldn't think twice about it, but I had no idea if he was gay or not. I suspected he was straight, making this even more awkward.

"Come here, we have to lay down and go chest to chest," Xavier said as he took my hand.

I knew we had to do this, but that didn't make it any less awkward and I knew I was going to be feeling weird about this when we got back to the classroom.

I went to my knees and then lay down with my chest against his. I couldn't help the hiss as his cold skin touched mine. I knew we would get warmed up soon enough, but until that happened it was going to suck. It also sucked because we were on the hard, cold ground. Typically, we would have a blanket or sleeping bag over us to help trap the heat, but we didn't have one. Which meant it would take longer for us to get warmed up, but it would help to fight off the risk of hypothermia at least. We might not get very warm, but it wouldn't kill us and that was really all I could hope for.

Xavier wrapped his arms around me and pulled me tight against his chest. Something I also didn't account for was the fact that we were the same height so we were chest to chest, but we were also cock to cock. And I didn't care how cold someone was, when they were naked and pressed up against another sexy naked person, their body notices.

Not good.

"I guess this would be a bad time to mention I'm gay," I said, letting out an awkward chuckle. It was a defense mechanism for me. When I was uncomfortable, I made jokes and said things I knew I shouldn't, but my brain/mouth filter didn't kick in to keep those words in my head.

"So am I."

Son of a bitch.

CHAPTER EIGHT

Xavier

"I GUESS THIS would be a bad time to mention I'm gay," Gage said with an awkward chuckle.

Yup, it would be a bad time to tell me the sexy naked man I was pressed up against was actually gay. It was fine when I thought he was straight. I survived the military without anyone discovering I was gay. I was very good at telling myself that everyone was straight and not allowing my body to respond to any touches or situations. All of that self-control went out the window though, once I knew they were gay.

I was also a bit annoyed that once again Jackson was right. He did say there was always at least one gay guy in the group. Of course, with my luck, it would be the guy that I was snuggling up with.

I had two options, either admit to being gay or tell him it was fine and play straight. The biggest issue with playing straight was the fact that I swore I wouldn't hide in a closet after I got out of the military. I swore I wouldn't live that life and even though it might be simpler to play straight right now, I didn't want to have to be back in that closet. Telling him

I was gay though, could have also added to the awkwardness of the situation. I was an asshole, but I wasn't as much of an asshole to make it so that only Gage was the one that was feeling uncomfortable.

"So am I."

Short and simple.

I wasn't going to tell him to not worry about it. I wasn't offering him any comforting words. I was simply letting him know that I was gay too and to not think about it. It was easier said than done though, because as every second that ticked by I was becoming painfully aware of his body pressed up against mine. I couldn't see it, but he felt very impressive to me. He was all muscle, hard muscle, and normally I liked my guys a bit smaller and leaner, but I had to admit he felt very good against me.

He moved his leg and it caused his cock to rub up against mine and I had to bite the inside of my cheek to keep the moan from escaping.

"Sorry, leg cramp," Gage said, and I had a feeling if I could see I would see a tint of red to his cheeks. I hated the flash of arousal that image brought to me. I was never going to get through this without getting hard. There was just no way.

"How old are you?" I asked. Maybe if we talked we would both be able to ignore the situation we were in.

"Twenty-five, you?"

Fuck, he was young. I thought he was closer to thirty. Most of the guys who come through this course are at least thirty. He had to be one of the younger ones that I'd had in this course.

"Forty-two. You start at eighteen?"

"Yeah. What about you?"

Eighteen was too young to be a firefighter, in my opinion. I knew it was a bit silly considering I went to war at eighteen, so why not be a firefighter that young. Still, having to run into burning buildings seemed a lot braver than going off to war to me, but that might have more to do with my feelings toward fire. I could do a lot of things, but the idea of running into a burning building made my chest tight. I had to give it to him, he had been doing this for seven years and he was still here, that's not easy.

"Four years now."

"Since you got out?"

"What?" I asked, confused.

Did he mean when I came out of the closet?

"The military. I can feel your dog tags, which are freezing by the way."

Oh, right. I forgot I had them on. I was so used to their weight that I didn't even recognize them anymore. "I was an Air Force pilot. When I got out I started working for the fire department."

"What was it like? The military, going to war?" he asked, and I could have sworn I heard a bit of worry and fear in his voice, but I wasn't certain why it would be there.

"It wasn't what I thought it would be. When you enlist everyone tells you what it's going to be like. Every recruiter, veteran, Boot Camp instructors, they all tell you that you are at risk of being shot, blown up, losing a limb or more, being captured and tortured. They don't hold anything back and even though I had been given plenty of warnings I still believed it wouldn't happen to me. I still believed that I was going to war and I would be fine. That I could come back home like nothing had happened. We all believed it. We were all stupid; young and stupid. The reality was that we were at war. I saw my friends being killed, some right next to me. I saw the worst that humanity had to offer and all the warnings in the world didn't prepare me for it."

This was the last thing I wanted to talk about and I shouldn't have been talking about it with him. He was a complete stranger and I didn't owe him the truth. I should have told him that it was fine and just like the media says, be all you can be, and all that shit. But for some reason, maybe it was our current position or the fact that we had deranged rednecks hunting us down, but I didn't want to lie to him. I didn't want to sugar coat the experience, even though I probably should have.

"That had to be extremely hard. I don't think extremely hard even covers it. I'm sorry you had to go through all of that," he said, and I could hear the sincerity in his voice. I also could have sworn it shook slightly, but I chalked that up to the shivers that were wreaking havoc throughout his body.

"I got through. A lot of guys didn't and I even made it out with all of my parts. I got nothing to complain about. Have you always wanted to be a firefighter?"

I was fully expecting him to give me the same answer I had received hundreds of times. *'Yes, I have always wanted to help people.'* It was the politically correct and acceptable answer, but I also knew nine out of ten times it was complete bullshit. Most people had a deeper reasoning for becoming a firefighter. There had to be a real reasoning behind choosing a career that involved running into burning buildings and it wasn't because you wanted to help people. I'm not saying they didn't want to help people, but that wasn't what drove them into the career.

"I hate that question. In the Fire Academy we used to get asked that all the time. All of the other cadets always had this profound reason behind their decision. They came from legacies, or they had experienced a fire growing up, they volunteered in the burn unit at the hospital and wanted to help people.

Everyone had something that was special that drove them. Whenever it got to be my turn, I always felt like an idiot because I didn't have some profound, life altering event that drove me to the Fire Department."

That was surprising to me, because I really expected him to tell me the same line. I doubted he didn't have a reason, everyone had a reason, it just might not have sounded that important to him. Still, I wanted to know.

"What was it?"

A strong shiver went down his spine and it once again forced our cocks to rub against each other and neither one of us could hold back the soft moan that escaped from our lips. At least I wasn't the only one who was struggling with our proximity.

Despite my better judgment, I held him closer against my chest, putting our hips closer together as well, but I was hoping it would help to produce more body heat between us. I was ignoring the warmth that went through my chest when Gage curled up closer into me.

"My brothers," he said, but it was slightly muffled with his face being turned into my chest.

"They were firefighters?" I asked, hoping for some clarification.

"No, they were eleven. Our mom got blood cancer when I was sixteen, stage three. They told her she was most likely going to be dead within the year, that it was a highly aggressive strand. She held on though, even when the doctors all told her she wouldn't make it, she would just tell them she had to make it for two more years. To do whatever they had to do, because she needed me to get to eighteen before she could leave this Earth. She made it though, one week after my eighteenth birthday she died."

The pain was clear in his voice. This wasn't an easy topic for him to talk about. It was still painful to him and I didn't blame him. I lost my parents in a forest fire, but I was an adult. I had been raised by them for the majority of my life. I was lucky in that sense. But Gage didn't get that luxury or privilege.

"Where was your dad?"

"Me and the twins have different fathers. Mine was never around, took off the second he discovered my mom was pregnant. The twins, their father stuck around until they were five before he took off. It was just us."

"Jesus, there was no one else to help. Grandparents, aunts or uncles?"

"Nope, just us. I did what I could. I made sure to help with the twins, get them meals, get them to school, and help with homework. I was old enough to work, so I would work as much as I could while trying to go to school and act like everything was fine. We were always worried about Social Services being called if anyone suspected anything was going on. The last thing we wanted was for any of us to be put into foster care. They would have split us up, including the twins, not to mention the horror stories we had heard about foster care. It was hard, but we made it work."

Holy fuck.

I never in a million years would have figured he had a troubled past. He didn't come across as someone who had struggled. I knew I shouldn't be judging people, but often I was right. My gut instinct was usually right on the money, but this time around it was wrong; so very wrong.

"So you went into the Fire Academy for them?"

"Yeah. I barely made it through high school. I'm not book smart. I missed a lot of school and I didn't do well on tests. I just barely made it through and I'm fairly certain some of my teachers gave me a passing grade just so they wouldn't have to deal with me again. I knew I needed a really good job though, to take care of the twins properly. Without it, we were still at risk of them being taken away from me. The Fire Academy was in need of recruits. It was good pay, better than minimum wage at some fast food joint. Plus there were health benefits and life insurance so the twins would have been taken care of if I died. It made the most sense to sign up."

As a father, I understood exactly why he signed up to be a firefighter. It gave him the financial stability that he needed to properly take care of his brothers who were more like his sons. I got it and I would have done the same thing. What bothered me though, was the fact that he shouldn't have had to do that. He shouldn't have had to care for his sick and dying mother and take care of his brothers. He didn't really get to be a kid himself and that was sad.

"I think you doing that for your brothers was the best reason anyone could have. And you must have enjoyed it, you've been in for seven years."

"I do enjoy it. I wasn't certain at first if I would, but I do love the work. I love the guys that I work with. I feel good about what I do at the end of the day and that's what I want for the twins."

"That's all any parent can hope for."

I was hoping that Dexter would find something he was passionate about later on in life when it was his turn to get a career. I was hoping he could do whatever he loved and be proud and happy to go to work every morning. I just wished I would get to be there for him, to experience it with him.

Gage was quiet for a bit, long enough that I couldn't help but wonder if he fell asleep. He proved me wrong though, when his muffled voice hit my ears.

"Though, when I signed up for the Fire Academy, I had no idea that one day I would be snuggled up naked to one of my instructors stranded in the woods being hunted by extremists. They should probably have put that on the welcome brochure."

I couldn't help the small chuckle that escaped. He was annoying and frustrating, but I had to give it to him, at times he was funny.

"You should have read the fine print."

"That fine print can be a bitch. I have to say though, out of all of the instructors that I have laid naked with, you are by far the biggest," he said and I could feel his smile against my chest.

I was surprised by the spark of jealousy that shot through my chest for a moment before it disappeared. I had no reason to be jealous. I didn't see Gage like that. He wasn't even my type.

"And exactly how many instructors have you laid naked with?" I shouldn't have asked. The answer wasn't going to be one I wanted to hear, but I needed to hear it. I needed to hear that it was just one other instructor, that it was a reasonable number. It was irrational, because he meant nothing to me, and yet I needed to know.

"Five. I guess I don't have to tell you how many closeted men there are in the Fire Department."

"No, you don't."

Five. I guess that wasn't as bad as it could have been. I had slept with roughly twenty other instructors and Captains within the Fire Department. That also didn't include the dozens of random hook ups to go with it. It wasn't like I was a virgin either. We all had a past.

"You are definitely the coldest too," he added, and he wasn't wrong.

"So are you. We need to generate more body heat, but outside of doing some jumping jacks, I'm not sure what we could do."

I had a lot of fun ideas that we could do, but I wasn't about to suggest any of them to him. I felt his hips moving forward and our cocks rubbed against each other once more as he spoke.

"I can think of something that could generate body heat. Strictly in a life saving sense, of course."

He placed a kiss to the center of my chest and I knew exactly what he was thinking and I would be lying if I said I wasn't tempted. He was sexy, and it would generate some body heat, but we were also exhausted, our bodies were pushed to their limits, not to mention we had nothing for lube. Even though I knew all of that, my body was still responding to his, to the idea.

"If we did, and I'm not saying we are, but if we did it would be purely for medical purposes." It was a ridiculous statement, but it might be the only way I would be able to say no later if this was really good.

"What happens in the cave, stays in the cave," Gage easily agreed, and that was all I needed to hear.

I rolled us over so his back was against the cold ground. If he cared at all he didn't show it, because he opened his legs and made space for me between them. I covered his body with my own and the second our cocks touched we were both moaning.

It was cold, very cold, but I knew soon enough we would build up a bit of body heat.

We couldn't have sex, I had no lube and I was not about to have sex without it. That didn't mean we couldn't dry hump like teenagers.

I rolled my hips and started to rub our cocks together. We both moaned and he tangled his hands in my hair, pulling me down toward him.

The second our lips touched I took control of the kiss. His lips were freezing, but they were also soft. He felt amazing against me and I knew if I wasn't careful I would become addicted to him and that was something I couldn't allow.

I felt his tongue against my lips and I opened my mouth, allowing him to enter. The second his tongue touched mine though, I was right back in control and he simply submitted to me. I rolled my hips once again and our moans were swallowed up by the other.

I didn't even care if we got warm. All that mattered now was how incredible he felt underneath me. I could have frozen to death right then and there and been happy.

I switched from just rolling my hips against him to thrusting, a breathless moan escaping my lips at the pleasure that shot through my balls and up my cock.

Gage pulled back from the kiss and let out a deep moan too. He arched his back and it gave me perfect access to his neck. I trailed kissed all along his skin as I felt his legs wrap around my hips.

"Fuck, Xavier."

I could hear the desperate need in his voice and I felt the same. There was nothing I wanted more than to be buried inside of him. My body and my mind were screaming for it and it took every ounce of self-control that I had to keep myself from slamming into his tight hole.

"You feel so good," I said into his neck as I picked up the pace.

I could feel that we were both painfully hard and I knew it wouldn't be long before we were both coming. Under normal circumstances, I would have taken him into my mouth, but that wouldn't generate the body heat that we needed to try and stave off the cold until morning. I was going to have to settle for rubbing up against him.

I wished I could see him, could witness the look of pleasure all across his face. I was betting he looked beautiful when he came.

I felt his hands trailing down my back and squeezing my ass, trying to pull me even closer to him. I captured his mouth once more and he joined me by thrusting his hips up to meet mine, causing us both to give a deep moan as we edged even closer. If I had been more focused on our surroundings, I would have thought about the noise we were making and that it could alert the men currently hunting us.

Currently though, I wasn't thinking about that or anything other than the pleasure that was scorching through my body. I could feel Gage's breathing becoming hitched and I knew it wouldn't be much longer, which was good because I didn't know how much longer that I could hold on for.

After a few more thrusts against each other, I felt Gage's cock swell and pulse and he arched back with a deep moan, breaking the kiss as he came. Feeling his cock pulse sent me over the edge and I held still as my cum shot out and landed on his stomach. The fact that he had our cum mixed together on his stomach only made my cock pulse more. I would have loved to see it.

I placed my forehead down against his as we both fought to catch our breaths.

Holy fuck, holy mother fucking god.

That should not have felt that good. That felt better then most of the sex I'd had and we didn't do anything but rub against each other. My heart was racing. It was pounding so hard against my chest I thought it might actually break it.

"Fuck, I gotta start carrying around a packet of lube in my wallet for emergency purposes." I could hear the goofy smile across his face and he was definitely not wrong.

"I would have loved to feel you wrapped around my cock." I placed a few kisses along his neck and he leaned his head back giving me better access.

"Wrapped around your cock; try wrapped around my cock."

I pulled back and looked down at him. I wished once again that I could see him, for him to be able to see me. I had a feeling that should have been a conversation we had beforehand and outside of the darkness. It never even occurred to me that we could have both been tops. It made sense, though. He wasn't that small, certainly not a spinner, but he also wasn't that large either.

"I only top," I stated.

"I only top," he mimicked.

Well, fuck me.

"Maybe you're a switch and you don't know it."

I had no idea why I was even trying right now. Despite how amazing this short time was I was never going to be doing it again with him. It was no concern of mine that he was a top as well. And yet, I couldn't get my mind to tell my mouth to shut the hell up.

"I've never bottomed. That's just not something I've been interested in. What about you, I'm sure you could be a switch."

"Nope. I tried it once and hated every second of it. All I will ever be is a top."

"Looks like what happens in the cave

really will stay in the cave."

I couldn't tell if he was disappointed or not. It really would have helped if I could see his face and gauge his reaction.

Was he disappointed?

Was he secretly considering trying to be a switch so we could fuck?

Or worse, was he relieved?

The self-doubt was sinking in now and I knew if I didn't shut it down soon, I would go down the rabbit hole and that was the last place I could be right now. We were still at risk and I needed to be focused on that and not my fucked up head.

"We should try and get some rest. Once it's first light out we need to get moving," I said, looking to try and get the conversation off of what would never happen between us.

"How do you want to sleep?" I could hear the slight exhaustion seeping into his voice. We had exerted ourselves, had been all day, and now his body was starting to recognize just how tired he was. I was tired as well, but I was used to being tired and staying awake for days straight.

"We'll have to sleep chest to chest to keep our body heat up. Hopefully come morning our clothes will be somewhat dry and with any luck the sun will be out and the rain will stop."

"I didn't check the weather, but I didn't think it was supposed to rain much this week," he said as I rolled us so we were on our sides once again chest to chest. "Do you think they will still be looking for us?"

"Jackson will look for us come

morning, he might already be looking for us now with the Park Rangers. As for the rednecks, it depends how determined they are.”

I really didn't know if the rednecks would give it a rest or not. I didn't know what their goal was, if they thought we were spies or the military, they might keep searching for us so they had a totem they could hold for everyone to see to get what they wanted.

As for Jackson, I knew come morning when class started and we weren't there he would know something went wrong. He would start to search for us. He might know something was wrong already, it just depended. Sometimes he would text me to check in on me, but I didn't always respond. If he sent me a text and got nothing back from me he might not worry right away. He might assume I was getting drunk and not in the mood to chat.

We just had to make sure we made it through the night and then get to a Ranger lookout tower to the radio. We should be able to reach it tomorrow and be sleeping in our own beds tomorrow night. We just had to make it through the rest of this night first.

CHAPTER NINE

Gage

THE SOUNDS OF birds chirping brought me slowly back to the living. I was no stranger to lack of sleep, but I didn't want to be awake right now. I was exhausted and my whole body was sore. Not to mention I was cold as fuck.

For a moment, just a moment, I wondered where my blanket ended up, before my brain kicked back in and reminded me that I was currently laying naked, on the hard ground, in a cave, because a bunch of fucking insurgents with guns shot the helicopter down and tried to kill us. This right here was why I didn't *do* camping. Why I didn't go hiking. Because leave it to me and my shitty luck to find the only serial killer in the woods. Sure, they weren't serial killers, but they weren't friendly campers either.

I let out a soft groan as I started to move away from Xavier's chest. I wanted to spend a lot more time pressed up against him, but I knew we needed to get moving. Plus, we were both tops and that wasn't about to change. At least we would always have our time in the cave to remember.

My movement caused Xavier to wake

up and I felt his arms loosen around me. I slowly pushed myself up into a sitting position. My whole body was aching from the cold and hard ground. Not to mention the chopper crash and running through the woods for hours. It was going to be a few days before I would be able to move without feeling stiff.

I turned slightly so I could look out the cave and I was pleased to see that it was sunny out. The rain had stopped and based on the shadows the sun wasn't very high, just past sunrise I would imagine.

I forced my body to move as I stood and went over to my wet clothes. We had tossed them into two piles and looking back on it now it might have been better for us to lay them out flat. It was too late now though.

"Tell me it stopped raining." Xavier's

gravelly voice echoed against the cave walls.

"It has. The sun is out and hopefully it helps to dry our clothes the rest of the way."

He gave a groan as he sat up and looked over at our clothes. I could see that he had already figured out they weren't very dry, but walking around the forest naked wasn't an option.

I dug out my cell phone from my pocket, but I couldn't get it to turn on. I was really hoping it was dead and not that the rain had caused water damage.

"Is yours working?" I asked as I held my phone up.

Xavier moved over to his clothes and dug his phone out. "There's no service and I only have twenty percent on it. We need to head out and start making our way toward the Ranger Tower. They'll have a radio and I can get in contact with Jackson."

"How far do you think it is?" I asked as I started to get dressed. My jeans were damp and cold and they were not comfortable at all, but I had to put something on.

"I'm not too sure, but I'll have a better idea once I get my surroundings," he commented, getting dressed now as well.

I was hoping we weren't too far. We were both exhausted, sore and hungry, the last thing we needed was to be wandering aimlessly around in the forest.

Once we were dressed we headed out and the warmth of the sun felt good against my cold skin. I knew we also had to be careful with the sun. If it got too hot out we risked getting heat stroke. We didn't have any water and there was no guarantee we would come across a freshwater stream to drink.

"Okay, I think we're about six hours away from the tower. I know that ridge," Xavier said, as he pointed in the direction of a large rocky hill off in the distance.

Six hours, fucking great.

CHAPTER TEN

Gage

THE PAST THREE hours had been anything but pleasant. Our only saving grace was the fact that it hadn't started to rain again and so far there weren't any gunshots following us. Still, with nothing but walking to do for hours my mind was constantly racing with 'what if' scenarios.

I still wasn't over the bombshells that

my brothers dropped on me just hours before I was set to fly to California. I wasn't too worried about Asher. He was going to a horse ranch in Texas. As long as he didn't get kicked in the head by a horse he should be fine. He was physically fit and could handle the physical labor that came with a horse ranch. He wasn't that book smart, but he didn't need to be. He was great with animals and he was good with people and reading them. He was very social and a place like a horse ranch made a lot of sense for him.

It was Greyson that concerned me the most. He wasn't very physical; he didn't really have muscles. He was very book smart and that was a good thing, but it also made it harder for him to understand social situations. I suspected he was kissing the autism spectrum, but it wasn't anything we had tested growing up. The only reason he had come such a long way was because of Asher. They had compensated for each other. But now Greyson was going to be surrounded by alpha males who wouldn't appreciate him being gay, nor would they tolerate his slight lack of social skills. He wasn't that bad, but he didn't read social cues very well. He didn't know when to stop talking or that a rant about something scientific wasn't as enjoyable for the other people as he thought. And all of that was before you factored in him learning how to shoot a gun and going into a warzone. It wasn't going to end well. I could feel it in my bones.

"Army medics, they just stay on base right?" I asked, breaking the silence between us for the first time since we left the cave.

"No, the doctors stay on base. Medics are more like a hybrid of a paramedic and ER doctor. It's on the medics to keep the soldiers alive long enough for them to get to a doctor. They go out with their unit, they are trained to shoot and they help with the operations."

That was not what I wanted to hear, not even close to it. I had been telling myself that at least Greyson would be safe on base working in the infirmary. Only now that dream was just blown up. I wanted to talk Greyson out of it, but I knew I couldn't. It wasn't my place to convince him to choose a different career. Just like it wasn't anyone's place to convince me to not be a firefighter and even if someone tried to talk me out of it I wouldn't have listened. I would have still done what I felt was right and I knew Greyson would do the same.

"Why the interest?" Xavier asked as he looked back at me.

I hadn't been walking beside him this whole time. I needed some space to get my thoughts and emotions in order. Plus, being next to him, having his arm lightly brushing against mine, it was not going to help me keep my hands to myself.

"Thing One and Thing Two decided to drop a bombshell on me just before I left for the training."

"Thing One and Thing Two?" he commented with a small smirk and I couldn't help but roll my eyes.

"Yeah, I know, but in my defense when they were younger they acted a lot like them. Even dressed up as them for

Halloween one year. It stuck," I said with a small shrug before I continued. "They are identical twins, but they couldn't be any different. Asher, he's ninety-three seconds older than Greyson, and he's not too great at school. Greyson had pulled double duty on tests and exams a few times and he's the only reason Asher even graduated. But Asher, he's got a great heart. He loves people and animals. I figured he would go to a trade school, but instead he got a job at a horse ranch in Texas."

"What's wrong with that? I knew an Army buddy who retired and took over his family's horse ranch in Montana. It can be peaceful working with the horses."

"There's nothing wrong with it, it just came out of left field. He had never mentioned being interested in it. I had no idea he was even doing research and going on interviews for it. I was set to leave believing that I would be coming home in a month to two eighteen year olds and a messy house from all the house parties. Now Asher will be in Texas and Greyson, the smart one, the one who could be a surgeon and got a full scholarship to Harvard Medical School, he's going to be an Army medic."

"Ah," Xavier said with complete understanding to his voice, but I wasn't certain if he related to my position or Greyson's.

I stopped walking and placed my hands on my hips as I tried to catch my breath. We had been going up the side of a little rock mountain for roughly an hour now. I knew we needed to get to the top to reach the Ranger tower, and normally I would be okay with the physical work, but I was so exhausted and sore from yesterday that this hike was taking everything in me. At the sound of my footsteps faltering, Xavier turned to face me and I felt a bit of pleasure to see he was fighting to catch his breath as well.

"It's not that I have a problem with the military life. If Asher told me he was going to the Army, I would be worried, but it wouldn't be surprising. Greyson though, he's smart, too smart, to the point where social situations aren't always clear to him. And that's fine; he's always had Asher next to him to help guide him through the murky waters. But now he is going to be the skinny, smart guy, who is out and proud surrounded by alpha males. And he's not going to have Asher there to protect him, to shield him from the potential hurt."

And that was my biggest worry. Greyson was going to be tossed all alone into a world I didn't think he was fully prepared for. He wasn't going to have his protector. He wasn't going to have the one person who just understood him fully. He was going to be seeing the worst humanity had to offer and he would have to do that knowing he was an outcast. I highly doubted he was ever going to be one of the guys. He was too different and in a world like the military, that wasn't a good thing.

Xavier walked over to me and took my hand in his. The physical contact surprised me, because Xavier wasn't much for touching. Sure, we did plenty of touching last night but that was for survival. Ever since this morning, he'd gone out of his way to avoid any physical contact with me. I understood it. He had been through war and he was my instructor. It wouldn't look good for anyone to see us together, or even make assumptions about us. He was trying to go back to how things were before the cave and I understood it. It would be best for us to go back to how things were. It would just be simpler, plus he was never going to switch to a bottom and I knew that wasn't something I could do either. I had never done it before, but I had never had an interest in it either. So going back to being an instructor and student seemed like the best plan for both of us.

"I'm not going to lie, Boot Camp is going to be hard for him. If he survives though, he'll be placed in a unit and they will protect him. Medics are like royalty over there. They all go out of their way to protect their medics, because they are the rest of the unit's lifeline if shit goes wrong. They'll teach him everything they know in and out of the field. He'll be their kid brother and they will love him. He'll see horrific things, but you can help him learn how to deal with it in a healthy manner."

It was a nice thought. He painted this really nice picture, but I also knew that coming back after seeing war, it wasn't a pretty picture. I didn't know any veterans personally, but I did see the homeless on the street. Alcoholics and drug addicts, barely able to function all so they could forget about the horrors that they had seen. The fact that any veteran was able to hold down a job and have a somewhat normal life was beyond impressive to me.

The fact that Xavier was able to continue being a pilot after being at war was impressive. I didn't doubt for a second though he had demons lying underneath the surface. And it was those kind of demons that I didn't want for my sweet baby brother.

"I don't know if I can handle him being over there," I softly admitted.

"Not a lot of people can. My parents had a really hard time with it. My mother worried, but my father was angry with me for a long time. At first, I didn't understand why he was angry with me, but after I had Dexter I got it. I don't think I would be able to handle it if Dexter told me he wanted to be in the military. To know that he was overseas at war and I couldn't be there to protect him. It took my father a very long time to accept my decision and I made sure that I never talked to him about what I saw or went through over there. I kept my injuries hidden as best as I could from both of them."

That was exactly how I felt. Greyson would be going off to war and I would be left behind, unable to be there to make sure he was protected from physical and mental dangers. I didn't know how I was going to be able to focus on my job while he was overseas at war. I knew I didn't have a choice in the matter though. It was Greyson's life and I had to accept it and I was going to have to figure something out that allowed me to function at work, but I highly doubted I would ever be okay with his decision. I also didn't know if I wanted Greyson to keep injuries from me or if I wanted to know about them. I really wasn't sure which would be worse.

"We should, ah... we should get going," I managed to say.

I didn't like the idea of being vulnerable around Xavier. I needed to stay strong. I was always the strong one and I was not about to let that change. My brothers needed me, now more than ever, to stay levelheaded and be there for when they needed me. I couldn't do vulnerabilities and weakness, too much was riding on me staying stable and able to handle anything that came my way.

Xavier just gave me a small nod and I could tell he understood my need to move forward, both physically and from this conversation. I appreciated that he didn't try and push the subject.

He released my hand and continued on climbing up our rocky mountain. Letting out a sigh, I started to follow after him. We were hopefully halfway there and I was really wishing tonight I would be able to sleep in my own bed. For a course that was supposed to be fun, so far it had been anything but. I was really looking forward to continuing on with this course and hopefully, getting to the fun part. All I knew was that after all of this, if I didn't pass this course, I was going to lose my shit.

CHAPTER ELEVEN

Xavier

FINALLY! THANK FUCK.

It had been closer to seven hours since we left the cave and I was starting to second-guess myself about the location of the Ranger tower. The trees kept it hidden from the ground and I had to use my memory from being in the sky. I had been confident, but the longer it took us to reach it, the more my confidence started to waver.

We both started to climb up the endless number of stairs. I took pride in my physical abilities, but even I was exhausted at this point and I doubted if I could even make it to the top. I knew Gage was feeling the same, but I also knew we both wanted to get the fuck out of this forest and back to the station.

I could hear Gage's heavy breathing as he climbed up behind me. At least I was hoping that was his breathing and not my own I was hearing. I knew I hadn't stayed as fit as I had been while I was in the Air Force, but I didn't think I was this out of shape, not that hiking uphill for seven hours and climbing five hundred stairs was out of shape exactly, but at one point in my life this would have been nothing.

I also couldn't ignore that I felt like shit. My stomach wasn't too happy with me right now and I knew that had nothing to do with the lack of food and water. Ever since I left the military I had been drinking every night and on my days off. I hadn't had anything to drink for two days now and my body was feeling it. I didn't want to think about what that meant. I kept telling myself it was from exertion and not something worse.

By the time we reached the top and opened that door, neither one of us could have defended ourselves if we needed to. I heard Gage groan at the sight of us being alone, I knew he had been expecting for there to be a Ranger here, but I wasn't worried about it being empty.

"The Rangers rotate within the areas to keep watch. The radio will still work and that is all we need," I barely managed to say as I crossed the short distance over to the desk.

I knew there wouldn't be much there. The Rangers brought what they needed, so nothing was left behind. There was no food or water, no cot to rest on, just two chairs, a radio and some binoculars. The radio and chairs were all we needed to get the fuck out of here.

I collapsed down into the chair with Gage doing the same to the other as he gulped air into his lungs. I turned my attention to the radio and switched it on and tuned it into the frequency for the station.

I pressed down on the mic button and spoke. "Mayday, Mayday, this is Captain Xavier Cruz with aerial station nineteen. Over."

"Will it only reach Jackson?" Gage asked as he continued the war against his breathing.

"Anyone on the frequency."

"Where the fuck have you been, Cruz?" I couldn't help the smile at hearing Jackson's voice.

"Decided to take the scenic route with the rookie. We're held up at Ranger Tower two-three-five."

"I got Bird Eleven already in the air. They've been searching the area once you didn't return last night. They found the crash site by the last ping on the black box, but no sign of you. Is there a spot for landing where you are?"

"Negative, we're surrounded by thick trees and uneven ground. We'll have to do a repel extraction." There was no way that the chopper could land in this terrain.

They would have to drop a line and pull us up.

"A scenic tour and a repel extraction, you sure know how to keep a first date interesting," Jackson teased and I knew he was loving this.

"Do we really need to talk about some of the first dates you've been on?" I knew he was teasing me. I had saved his ass plenty of times when he was trapped by a fire. It was time he saved my ass. I was doing my best to ignore how my time with Gage ended last night. From some of the stories Jackson told me about his first dates, this didn't even hit his top ten.

"Are you guys injured?" Yeah, it was probably best that he changed the subject.

"We're fine. The bear only ate part of the rookie's leg," I said with a smirk as I glanced over at Gage. He didn't look impressed.

"It coulda ate something worse. Bird Eleven is going to meet you in thirty minutes just east of the tower. They'll drop a line down for you. Try not to get into a crash this time."

"Over and out," I said, before I pushed the mic back. I knew I was going to need to give him a full rundown on what happened, but that could happen later. I wasn't exactly in the mood to rehash shit.

"We have to repel up?" Gage asked, and I couldn't tell if he was worried or not over the fact. I doubted he had done something like that before. I knew it wasn't typically taught in the fire academy.

"It'll be fine. They'll lower down a harness and the rigging brings you back up. You'll be on the chopper within two minutes," I answered as I sat back and rubbed at my temples, trying to stave off the growing headache.

"I've taken the repelling course."

Of course he had.

It seemed like he was very interested in taking any course that would make him more skilled. He might not have had the typical reasoning for being a firefighter, but he took it very seriously all the same. He was dedicated and hard working, I had to give him that.

"We need to leave in twenty to make sure to get to the pick up location," I said as I closed my eyes, hoping that it would help ease my headache. I was starting to feel a lot worse now that I was sitting down and no longer moving. I just needed some sleep and then I would feel better, that's all this was.

"How old is Dexter?"

It took my mind a minute to even realize how he knew about Dexter. I almost never talked about him. It wasn't because I was ashamed to have a child. Dexter was the one thing I was most proud of. I didn't talk about him with people because it hurt. It hurt knowing that my only child hated me.

Dexter didn't know the truth and part of me wanted to tell him. I wanted to sit down with him and explain what had transpired between his mother and me. I didn't want him to hate me, but at the same time, I didn't want him to hate her either. I didn't want to take away the only parent he'd truly ever known.

I'd been with Kate and my son for the first six years of his life, but I was deployed for half of it and on operations in between. He barely saw me when I was there.

After the divorce when Kate was granted custody, I was devastated, but I also understood it. Part of me had started to doubt if I should be in Dexter's life at all, and not because I was ashamed of being gay, but because he was so used to me not being there. Maybe it would have been better for me to step away completely, so if I did die in the line of duty he wouldn't miss me as much. It wouldn't be such a devastating blow to him.

I'd made it a whole week before the pain of not speaking with him became too much. It didn't matter though, because Kate made sure we didn't get time together. The result was a soon to be seventeen year old who didn't know me and hated my guts because of what Kate had said to him about why I wasn't around.

I was trying to gain some footing with Dexter and I was really hoping that once he turned eighteen and became an adult it would be easier for us to communicate. I would be able to reach out to him without having to go through Kate. All of that was assuming he would even take my calls after his mother's brainwashing.

I knew when I was discharged from the Air Force I could have taken Kate back to court, but I was so screwed up, still am, and I didn't want to dump that on Dexter. And once again, Kate was the only parent he knew and I didn't want to take that from him by giving him the truth.

"He'll be seventeen in three months," I

answered as I kept my eyes closed.

"Sixteen, I remember being terrified for the twins to be that age. Mostly for Asher. I could always count on Greyson to be level headed and logical, but when Asher got going he was able to drag Greyson into some pretty wild shit."

I cracked my eyelids open just part way so I could look at him as I spoke. "It couldn't have been easy. Having to be a parent, but also a brother."

"It wasn't easy. There was a balance to it and I'm not too sure I even have that balance figured out now. Now though, it'll be a bit different, I guess. They are legal adults so I don't have to be a parent any longer, but I doubt I can just switch it off. I tried to remember growing up, especially once they got older, that they didn't always need a lecture. That sometimes they needed an older brother to bitch to or admit to doing something they shouldn't have done, but they wanted to brag about it."

"What was the worst thing you let them get away with?" I didn't have any stories of my own for Dexter, but I did like hearing them about other children. Some of the guys I worked with in the military used to show off pictures or videos of their children and for a little while I could pretend that it was my own son I was watching. I was well aware that it was pathetic and sad, but on those extremely hard days and lonely nights it was all I had to push me to keep going.

"I guess that depends on your definition of horrible. They did the typical teenager thing, the typical twin thing. Greyson would pretend to be Asher, mostly for tests or exams, like I said. There had been a few assignments when Asher was close to failing out that I would ask Greyson to write it. I know that counts as cheating, but I never put too much stock in grades. I knew Asher would find something he loved to do to make a career out of it. I didn't need them both to be lawyers or doctors."

"I knew a lot of guys who had the biggest heart and yet were dumb as rocks. Book smarts isn't everything."

That was also something Kate and I disagreed on. She came from a family that expected you to get the highest grades every time. I remember one time she got a B+ on a math test and she cried, almost had a panic attack at just the thought of showing her parents. I never wanted that for Dexter. School was supposed to be fun, a chance for you to learn, but also discover different pieces of yourself. It wasn't supposed to be about turning children into stressed out freaks and ticking time bombs.

"I've always told them that they didn't have to be the smartest person in the room, they just had to be in the room. They snuck out a couple of times, went to parties, came home drunk, typical teenage rebellion. I guess the biggest thing they pulled was when they were seventeen and both dated the same guy without telling him."

"What?" I couldn't have heard that right.

Gage smiled at the memory and I could tell he was slightly proud of it. "The twins are gay. We used to joke around about how our mother must have had this special gene that she passed onto us or something. Asher has always been a social butterfly and by the time he was sixteen he had already had sex and multiple boyfriends. Greyson was the exact opposite. They liked the same guy though, Matt, and he liked a bit of both of them. Asher went out on date with him first and when he got home he told Greyson that he should go on the next one. From there, it snowballed into them both dating Matt and Matt having no idea. It lasted about six months before Matt started to date the head cheerleader."

"High school has gotten far more complicated than I remember." None of that shit certainly happened when I was in school. Apparently it was a good thing that Dexter didn't have a twin brother, because I couldn't imagine what they would have done together.

"Well, that makes sense. You didn't even have the Internet back then."

There was that fucking smirk again. I didn't know if I wanted to slap it or kiss it off his face. Neither were going to happen, so I changed the subject.

"We should start making our way to the pick up location. We're both sore and exhausted, so it might take us longer to reach the extraction point than normal."

I didn't really want to get up and move, but I knew we needed to. Staying here definitely wasn't an option. Whether we liked it or not, we had to start making our trip to the extraction point and that would bring us one step closer to the station.

One step closer to my apartment where I could shower and sleep.

Gage just gave me a nod and I could

tell he wasn't happy about it either, but if we wanted out of this forest we had to move. Pushing my sore body up and out of the chair was not easy, but I forced myself to ignore the stab of pain. Just like I forced my mind to not think about how the room spun slightly or how my head pounded more fiercely as I stood.

Far more slowly than I would ever admit, we climbed down from the Ranger tower and arrived at the extraction location. I could hear the *whomp whomp whomp* of blades of the chopper in the near distance. It was a sound that brought a great deal of comfort to me, because the thumping sound indicated safety. Usually when I heard it, I was going to help rescue good men and women. I was in control, even though I couldn't control everything within my surroundings. I couldn't control how the enemy troops would react, but I could control how I responded to them. I could control my landing, my flight path, and rescue maneuvers. When I was in that cockpit, I had control and there was a great sense of safety in that.

I knew that wasn't how all veterans felt. A majority of them hated the sound because it triggered painful memories. I could also understand why they felt that way. Often when troops on the ground needed air support it was because everything was going to shit. People were hurt, shot, blown up, you name it. It only made sense that the sound of propellers could send someone into a spiral.

The wind picked up around us as the chopper hovered above. I could see the side panel being opened and I knew it would only be a minute before they started to send the repel gear down.

I glanced over at Gage to see how he was handling all of this. It was one thing to do it in a class and another to do this in real life. He was holding strong though. I wasn't seeing any fear in his eyes. He appeared to be calm and steady, a good sign. Once the harness was close enough I reached up and grabbed it, looking over to Gage as I spoke.

"You're going first." He went to argue, but I wasn't having any of it. I was the instructor and he was the cadet. "That's an order."

He wasn't happy about it, but I didn't care. We were going back to the station and that meant we were going back to how things were supposed to be. I was his instructor, his superior and he was the cadet. I needed to put that defining wall back up between us and there was nothing that he could do or say to bring it back down.

Gage easily hooked the harness onto himself and I waved up to let the guys know to start bringing him up. I stood there and watched as Gage ascended into the late afternoon sky. It was getting hotter out and I could feel the exertion within my body. There was a slight tremble now and I knew I needed to get some water and rest soon before I couldn't fight it off.

I watched as Gage was secured within the chopper and the harness was lowered back down to me. The second I could reach it, I was slipping it on and the ground beneath me started to disappear. I kept my eyes up on the chopper. Looking down never bothered me before, but I knew today would be different. With the way my body was feeling, the way my stomach was feeling, I wasn't going to risk a dizzy spell or losing what little was left in my stomach. The second my feet touched down on the metal floor of the chopper, I felt like I could take my first real breath since the crash.

"You all right, Cruz?"

That was Smith; he was one of the older pilots. He had been working for the fire department for close to twenty years now. He always said he wouldn't retire unless he lost his sight or hearing. The guys often joked around about having to pry the stick from his cold dead hands. They had no idea how accurate that was though. Losing your ability to fly was a lot like a biker losing his ability to ride his motorcycle. It wasn't something that any pilot wanted to experience.

"Fuckers shot my bird," I answered as I made my way over to the other seat in the front. If I couldn't fly, then I damn well was still going to be sitting in the front.

"We gotta do something about those assholes."

"Jackson will make the call." I didn't know what Jackson was going to do. I doubted the police would do anything and then that fell to the Feds, but what they were going to do, I had no idea. They were in a tight spot, because they couldn't go in guns blazing and end up on the five o'clock news. The survivalists had every right to defend their property. The issue came when they believed everyone flying over them were spies. I didn't know what the procedure was in that situation, but I knew it would be on Jackson to figure it out.

"Anything feel broken?"

A quick glance over to Gage told me he was still holding strong. He was sitting with his back against the back of the chopper. He had his eyes closed and his breathing was even. I wasn't too sure if he was asleep or just resting. I was leaning toward resting based on the slight furrow of his brow, presumably from the pain he had to be feeling.

I turned my attention back to the windshield and spoke. "We're fine. Just banged up. I was able to control the crash landing as well as could be expected."

"No one was too badly hurt, that's the best outcome you could hope for. We'll be back soon and then you can get some grub and sleep."

That was all I wanted right now, sleep and a shower. I knew I should eat something, but the queasiness of my stomach was telling me it wouldn't be the best idea. I needed some water and then I could always eat later after getting some sleep. We just needed to get to the station and then I could get the fuck home.

CHAPTER TWELVE

Xavier

THE SECOND WE touched down I was climbing out of the chopper and making my way toward Jackson as he stood on the outside boundary of the designated chopper pad. I could see a mixture of anger and worry over what happened to us. I didn't need him to worry about me though. I was more than capable of taking care of myself, even in the forest.

"Something has to be done about the survivalists. Nothing tragic happened this time, but it was close. They didn't just shoot us down, they came to the crash site and started to shoot at us," I said, before he had a chance to open his mouth.

"Graze or a through and through?" he asked with a nod to my arm.

"Graze, I can take care of it myself. The cadet is fine, just banged up a bit."

"I'll make sure he gets looked at before sending him to the dorm. Go get yourself taken care of. I'll make the calls to see what can be done about the survivalists."

That was all I needed to hear. Without looking toward Gage, I made my way toward the side of the station so I could go around to get into my truck. The second I was sitting in it, I couldn't help but close my eyes and rest my head back. I could feel my whole body trembling and I knew I had to get to my apartment before I wasn't able to drive.

"You're just tired, that's all," I told myself, not ready to admit what was really going on. I knew the signs, fuck, I had seen them myself in other soldiers and vets, but this wasn't that. Nope. I was just tired after everything that happened, that's all.

Turning my truck on, I pulled out of the station and started to make the drive to my place. Thankfully, it was only a twenty minute drive away.

The second I arrived home, I stumbled out of my truck and headed for the door. Sweat was starting to run down my face and I felt like I was going to hurl any second. Once I made it to my door, I pulled out my key and had to fight to get my hand to stop shaking long enough to get the key into the hole.

Slamming the door behind me, I didn't even think, I just went into my kitchen and grabbed the half drank bottle of whiskey sitting on my counter. I unscrewed the lid and took a drink right from the bottle. I knew it wouldn't be instant, but I also knew within a moment or two I would start to feel a bit better.

I took another swig before I sank down to the floor and placed my head against the cupboard. Closing my eyes, I decided to ride it out and see if my theory was right or not. I was praying I was wrong, that it wasn't alcohol withdrawal, because that meant I had gone and gotten myself addicted to the booze.

I knew I drank a lot, and frequently, but I didn't think my body was becoming dependent on it. I had been foolish to think I could drink for years straight without a single issue. I had fooled myself into believing there wasn't a problem because I didn't need to drink to get through the day, I just did it at night. After all, people have a beer or two after work; it was natural.

I liked getting drunk; it helped me sleep. It helped me keep the nightmares at bay. It was either drink or take a sleeping pill and those were addictive, so surely a drink was better.

But as my body started to feel better I knew just how stupid and naive I had been, because I got addicted to alcohol all the same and now that I knew about it, I had no idea what I was going to do.

CHAPTER THIRTEEN

Gage

I SHOULDN'T HAVE been surprised that Xavier left without even saying a word to me, but I was. And I hated that I was a little hurt by it. I knew we had to go back to being instructor and cadet, but I didn't think he would be able to forget about the night we spent together that easily.

Again, I knew it was foolish, because

what we did was out of necessity. We had to generate body heat and that was the best way. Still though, with how amazing it felt, I thought he felt it too. I thought he felt the same connection that I did, but apparently not. That was fine. We both had different lives. We both lived on opposite ends of the country. Not to mention we were both tops and I would never switch. Xavier was right. It was better to pretend like it never happened.

I immediately went and walked down toward the dormitory. I knew technically I should be heading to class, it was my second day and there was still work I needed to pick up that I had missed, but fuck it, I could catch up tomorrow. Today was going to be about me and that meant a shower, water, food and sleep. Everything else was tomorrow's problem.

The dormitory for this station was not connected to the actual station, but rather in its own building roughly a hundred feet from it. I had only been in the dormitory for a few minutes yesterday, just long enough to drop my bags off and head to the station. I will say it was much nicer than I was expecting. There was a large cooking area with some standard food in it, coffee, milk, eggs, cereal, bread, hamburger buns, frozen burgers, and hot dogs. If we wanted something different we could head into town, roughly a fifteen minute walk, to grab it. According to Jackson, there was some great pizza in town that I was going to have to try tomorrow.

As for my room, I was in a double room, but I didn't have a roommate. The dormitory was often used for a full fire academy and specialized courses in between seasons. It meant we were all lucky enough to be able to have our own room and our bathroom. The bathroom was connected to each room and it was designed to help with the flow when the dormitory was full. It was nice, almost like a hotel room. There was even a desk to do work at. Until tomorrow though, my room would be very much a hotel room. I was planning on doing nothing but eating and sleeping.

I went over to the fridge in the kitchen to see if there was anything I could grab to eat real quick. I snagged a water bottle from the shelf in the door and took a long drink from it before I turned my attention to the food. I saw a styrofoam to-go container with a note sitting on top of it. My name was written on the folded piece of paper. I picked it up and saw some pretty shitty handwriting, but I was able to make it out.

We figured after the long night you had you could use some real food. Hope you like Chinese.

-The Guys

Okay, that right there was exactly why I loved being in the Fire Department. It was a brotherhood that reached from one end of the world to the other. It didn't matter what you looked like, who you dated, where you lived, rich or poor, none of it mattered because you were a brother to millions, it was just that simple. We all looked out for each other and we all wanted to ensure that everyone was taken care of. It was this simple act that made everything that happened within the past twenty some odd hours better.

I grabbed the food and opened it up to see that it was rice, honey garlic chicken, and cooked vegetables. It smelled amazing, even though it was cold. I wasn't picky when it came to food. We didn't always get to have much growing up, so I never turned any down. Asher and Greyson were the same, but Greyson was starting to get a bit picky. He didn't want to eat things he didn't enjoy or appreciate the taste. I could understand that though. If you didn't really get to eat the foods you liked growing up, it only made sense to seek them out as an adult. Thankfully, Asher was like a garbage disposal and ate anything that was in front of him.

After warming my food up, my mouth watering as the smell hit my nose, I grabbed a fork before I made my way toward my room. I needed to shower, but

I was planning on eating first.

I sat down at the desk and took a bite. I couldn't contain the groan that escaped me at the taste that flooded my mouth. Fuck, this might be the best thing I'd ever eaten.

I pulled my cell phone out and tried to see if it would turn on, but it didn't. I couldn't remember what battery percent it was at when I got onto the chopper so there was a chance that it had just died and it wasn't water-logged. I would have to put it into some rice just in case before I plugged it in. If there was water inside of it, trying to charge it could short circuit the system. It would be better to play it safe.

I got up and grabbed my laptop from my bag. I needed to check in with the twins and make sure they were okay.

They were going to text me last night to let me know that they were okay but obviously I didn't get that text with a dead phone. I knew they would be packing up their stuff and getting ready to leave shortly. I hated that I wouldn't be there for them, to see them off. I wanted to be there. I would have taken them to the airport. Hell, I would have taken them all the way to their new lives if they had let me. I understood it was bad timing on all of our parts, but if I knew that they weren't going to be home when I got back, I wouldn't have left. I could have taken the course another time and at least been there for what little time we had left. Instead, now I was going to be returning to an empty house, for the first time in my entire life, and I had no idea how I was going to handle the quiet when I got home. There was normally always noise in the house. Sometimes it was Asher's country music blaring and other times it was the sound of their footsteps as they walked back and forth to each other's room.

It took about a year after our mother's death before I moved into her room so they could each have their own. They appreciated the privacy, but often you could find them together in one of their rooms. The house had never really been quiet and after a bad day it was nice to come home to the noise.

There had been plenty of times where I would crawl into bed with them and hang out. Being around the twins helped to calm the demons that a job like mine could bring. And now I was going to have to find a new way to deal with those demons, a healthy way.

I couldn't risk becoming dependent on alcohol to get me through the day. I had seen that plenty of times with guys that had been on the job a long time. They got drunk the second they could when their shift was done. I didn't want that life. I was going to have to figure it out.

I opened my email and ignored every one that didn't have one of my brothers' names on it. They hadn't sent me an email. I figured they wouldn't have. They would have just texted me, but if I didn't reach out to them they would worry that something had happened to me.

I quickly sent them off an email letting them know my phone got wet and I was drying it out. I wasn't going to be telling them about what happened, it would only make them worry and that was the last thing I wanted.

With that done, I browsed around online while I ate before finally grabbing some clean clothes and headed into the bathroom. I turned on the water as hot as it could go without burning my skin before I stripped out of my dirty clothes and stepped under the spray.

The second the water hit my skin I was in heaven. It felt amazing against my cold and battered body. I could have stayed here for hours, but I knew that wouldn't be possible because I would get light-headed and potentially pass out, something I didn't want to happen. I allowed the water to wash over me for a few minutes longer before I started the process of getting all of the dirt and grime off of me. I swear it felt like there was actual slime on my skin.

After a thorough cleaning, I washed my hair and when the struggle to keep my eyes open became too great, I turned the water off and quickly dried off. I didn't bother with much of my clothes outside of my boxers before I headed over to my bed. The curtains were pulled back over the small window so I didn't have to worry about the sunlight shining in. I was hoping by the time I woke up it would be tomorrow morning or at least close enough to it.

I pulled the covers off and collapsed onto the bed. It was so incredibly soft, especially compared to the cave floor that made my bed last night. I had to admit though, I missed the cold body that had been pressed up against me.

CHAPTER FOURTEEN

Xavier

"COME ON, PICK up," I whispered to myself as I headed down the hallway toward the classroom.

The sound of an endless ring was something I had come to associate with my son. Every time I called Dexter that was the only sound that greeted me. I knew he was never going to answer, he never did. I would leave him voicemail after voicemail, but he never returned my calls.

I wished I could get through to him. I felt like if I could just talk to him, then I could start to repair the damage that had been done. I knew Kate had told him a shitload of lies about me and I wasn't going to be able to start to disprove them until I could get Dexter to speak with me.

I wasn't blaming everything on Kate. I had made plenty of mistakes myself where Dexter was concerned. I shouldn't have given up fighting for him. I should have changed career paths in the Air Force so I could be home more and would have stood a better chance at getting joint custody of him, or at the very least a set visitation schedule instead of it being left up to Kate. It would have been messy and frustrating at the best of times, but I would have had a better relationship with my son. It was a regret that I was going to have to carry with me for the rest of my life and it was time I tried to correct that wrong.

"You have reached the voicemail box of Dexter Cruz. Please leave your name and a brief message and he will get back to you as soon as possible."

I knew it was irrational to feel hatred toward an automated voice messaging system, but every time I heard that bitch's voice I wanted to punch her in the face. "Dex, it's your Dad. I would really like for you to call me back so we can talk. Please, Son, call me back."

I hit the end button before I pocketed my phone. I had no faith that Dexter would call me back, he never did, but it was a call I was going to make every day until I could finally talk to him. If there was one good thing that came from the shitshow that was the past forty-eight hours, it was that I needed to make things right between Dexter and I. I could have died in those woods and I never would have gotten to tell my son that I loved him. I wouldn't have gotten to hug him one last time, to hear his voice. I had to make this right, no matter what it took.

I walked into the classroom to see that the cadets were already there. They were talking amongst themselves and I instantly scanned the room and found the one person I wanted to see more than anything. Gage. He was speaking with a couple of the guys around him from where he sat in the front row.

I don't know why, but him sitting in

the front row surprised me. I knew he hadn't done well in school and I had assumed that meant he would naturally place himself in the middle or at the back of the room. Out of the way so he could blend in and go unnoticed like I was certain he had done growing up.

I was a man that could admit when I was wrong and I was wrong in my assumptions of Gage. I thought he was too young to be here, that he would be too immature. When in reality he might be more mature than I was. It took a special person to step up at a very young age and raise not one but two children. He gave up the rest of his childhood for his brothers and that was one of the most honorable things I had ever heard of. There was depth to Gage and I shouldn't be interested in him, but I couldn't stop thinking about him.

I'd never done anything with any of the cadets that I trained. I'd always kept it professional and kept a wall up between us. Shit, I was like that with people I worked with each and every day. For a couple of reasons; one, I didn't like to bring any unnecessary drama into my life. Sleeping with someone that you worked with had the potential for disaster. And two, firefighters got killed all the time. Every single time we went out for a call it could be the one that took our life. I had enough loss in my life. I couldn't handle having another one. I couldn't handle losing someone that I potentially could care deeply for. It was easier for me to keep things simple and without emotions. Gage had the potential to stir up emotions within me and that was dangerous.

Thankfully, we were both tops and he had no interest in bottoming. We weren't compatible, making it an easy clean break between us.

Or so I tried to convince myself.

Jackson nudging me with his elbow brought me out of my thoughts and I snapped my eyes away from Gage's radiant smile. Looking over at Jackson, I could see the smirk on his face and I already knew what he was going to say before he even opened his mouth.

"Found the one gay guy in the group, eh?" he teased, and I had to fight down my irritation.

"He is gay, but that wasn't why I was looking at him. I was making sure he looked ready to be back. A night in the woods with gun-toting extremists after you might have been what broke him. I don't need an unstable cadet up in the air with me."

I was not about to give Jackson the satisfaction of seeing me checking anyone out. And he was never going to hear about what happened between us in the cave. That was going to stay between Gage and me. At least I hoped it would. He could have already spilled the beans to the other cadets, but I was hoping he would have enough respect for himself as well as me to keep it quiet.

"Eventually, you are going to have to accept that you are capable of caring for someone. That being attracted to a guy doesn't automatically put a target on their back," Jackson countered without any malice to his voice. I knew he was trying to help, but right now I was not in the mood for it.

"Says the man who sleeps with multiple guys at once and doesn't take any relationship seriously. You are the last person that gets to give life advice." I couldn't keep the edge from my voice. I was still too raw from not being able to talk to Dexter, plus my discovery about myself last night.

I was still in denial about my dependency on alcohol. My mind knew the signs. My mind understood what my body was feeling, but I still refused to believe it. I couldn't be addicted to alcohol, that just wasn't possible for me. Lots of people drank every day. It would be natural for me to feel sick after exerting myself for two days in the woods. We didn't have any water or food, we barely slept and we were freezing. It was perfectly natural for me to have felt like shit last night. There was nothing more to it than that. I continued to give myself every excuse in the book, determined to believe at least one of them.

"Maybe I just haven't found the man that can hold my attention long enough to change my life," he countered, slightly offended, which I wasn't too sure as to why. This wasn't the first time we'd talked about his man-whoring ways. It had never bothered him in the past; it didn't bother him three days ago. I couldn't help but wonder what had changed.

I didn't ask him though, that would have taken our friendship to a more personal level and that wasn't something I was looking to achieve. Friends also get killed and I had buried enough friends to last me three lifetimes. The only way to avoid having to bury someone else that I cared for was to make sure I never cared for anyone ever again.

"You hear back from the police about our woodland rednecks?" I asked, looking to change the subject to something we were both more comfortable with.

Jackson gave a snicker at that. "I put the call in to the Sheriff's office and they were going to work with the Park Rangers to try and come to some sort of a solution. Obviously, they don't want to cause open season on each other, but the Sheriff can't let them shoot down choppers and go on a hunting party for survivors. If they aren't able to come to a peaceful solution, then they won't have any choice but to bring in the Feds. It's something they are avoiding though, for obvious reasons."

The Feds getting involved would turn it

all into one epic clusterfuck. The extremists would take it as an act of terrorism against their people and their beliefs. They would start shooting and trying to kill as many Feds that they could. They would make a show of it and demand to have news reporters there to watch as the Government tried to take away their rights and put their women and children in harm's way.

"Their encampment is in our training flight path. I'm going to have to change the training area to ensure we don't fly over them and risk getting shot down again. We got lucky this time around."

And that was really what it came down to.

Fucking luck.

If the impact to the chopper had been on the engine and not the tail, we could have blown up before we even reached the ground. If I hadn't been able to control the landing as well as I did, we could have blown up on impact. We got lucky and I wasn't foolish enough to believe that we would get lucky a second time. I would need to change the training area to ensure that the cadets were safe when we were in the air.

"Agreed. You can map that out today while I go over the weather forecast with them."

I gave him a nod and we both moved over to the front of the class so we could get it started. I would need to find the best place in the opposite direction of the extremists encampment where we could safely do the training. The original flight path gave us the most level and open ground, making it safer for the cadets to repel down and get used to repelling people up, but it wasn't an option any longer and I might need to change how we did things moving forward.

"Good morning," Jackson started. "We are going to focus on reading forecast maps this morning and getting you guys used to predicting the wind direction. This will help you to have a better understanding of how a fire will move, but also if you are going to be repelling victims up to the chopper, you need to know how the basket or harness is going to swing."

One of the cadets further in the back raised a hand and Jackson gave a nod, indicating for him to speak. "Are we still going up in the chopper after it was shot down?"

"Yeah, what is stopping that survivalist

group from doing it again?" another cadet added.

It was reasonable for them to be concerned with being shot down. They didn't sign up for that and it wouldn't be something that they would be used to experiencing. It pissed me off that they were worried about their safety when they were up in my rig. I had always worked my ass off to make sure that the people who go up with me are as safe as they can be. And now the people that were supposed to put their lives in my hands were scared about getting back onto my rig.

It was bullshit.

I couldn't help but glance over to see Gage's reaction. I wanted to pull him aside and talk to him, check in to see how he was feeling after the last two days, but

I knew I couldn't do that. Any alone time with him would be dangerous and far too tempting.

Gage's eyes locked with mine and I felt a wave of heat overtake me. This man had the potential to be dangerous and I really needed to keep the distance between us. Something that wouldn't be easy with us being up in the air together again. I had to make sure my walls were up around him, that I didn't let my body and desire blind me from the reality of the situation.

It wasn't even that he was much younger than me. It was the fact that our lives were on two different paths. He had a whole career back in Baton Rouge and I had a life here that I couldn't walk away from. Dexter was here and even if we weren't speaking with each other, I wasn't going to leave and abandon him here.

Even if I was willing to entertain the idea of starting something with Gage, I knew the relationship would be doomed before it even got off the ground.

I broke the eye contact with him and turned my attention back to the cadets who had voiced their concerns. "I will be creating a new flight path that we will use for any training, one that will take us in the opposite direction of the encampment. The Sheriff and the Park Rangers are also working together to try and resolve the issues that the survivalists have."

"We are doing everything within our power to ensure your safety while you are in the air," Jackson added.

I could see that they were still worried about it all, not that I could blame them, but they were at least relieved to hear that we had a plan and things were being done to prevent this situation from happening again. With no further questions, Jackson got started on the lesson and I headed out to work with the maps to try and find a safe route that would work for the course. Somehow, I knew it was going to be a long ass day.

CHAPTER FIFTEEN

Gage

THE MUSIC FROM the bar was blaring even through the closed door.

The day had been pretty long with nothing but class work. I couldn't even count the number of forecast maps that I had seen today and my mind was in desperate need of a break. It had been a long time since I had to sit in a classroom for eight hours straight. Even in the academy we had time outside of class while we worked on the practical aspect of the job.

I hadn't realized until today how desperately I had needed that time outside of the classroom in order to make it through the class work. I was fairly decent at reading a forecast map, but as each one grew in difficulty it was harder for me to see what Jackson was talking about. It was harder for me to not let my insecurities about my intelligence seep in and I wasn't confident that I had managed to fight them off fully. When the guys had suggested that we go and let off some steam at one of the few local bars, I jumped on it.

It was nearing ten o'clock at night and I knew it would be too late to call Greyson over in Georgia, but I figured it wouldn't be too late for Asher in Austin. He was normally a night owl to begin with and I doubted the last couple of days had changed that. I hadn't been able to talk to them since I left and I was going through a sense of withdrawal without hearing their voices. They had emailed me back just letting me know they were still alive, but they didn't get into any details about how things were going with them and I was very anxious to hear all about it. I was going to have to try and find some time tomorrow to speak with Greyson, even if I had to leave class for fifteen minutes to catch him.

I pulled out my phone, very thankful that it was working, and called Asher. After a few rings he answered, but the tired-sounding voice did not go unnoticed.

"You know it's almost midnight here and I have to be up at six, right?"

Hearing the sound of his voice instantly had me smiling. I knew I should have said that I was sorry and that he could call me tomorrow so he could sleep, but I just needed to talk to him for a few minutes. To hear the slight rough tone to his voice that always told me it was Asher. They were identical twins, but there was a slight difference to their voice. Asher had a slight gruff to his tone whereas Greyson's voice was smooth like silk.

"Sorry, I just wanted to hear your voice. It's been five days since I've seen you guys."

To some I knew five days would be nothing, but to me it felt like years. I had been around them their whole lives. Every single day I was there, taking care of them, and now I had been away from them for five days and I felt a great sense of loneliness. I had no idea how I was going to adapt to living alone once I returned. I knew I could get a roommate or something, but that would take one of the rooms away from the twins when they came home for visits and I didn't want to do that. I wanted them to know that no matter how much time had passed or where they were in life, that they could always come home. That they always had a place to live with me.

"You miss the insanity already?" Asher asked, sounding a bit more awake.

"I'm always going to miss you guys. How have you been? What has it been like working on a ranch? Are the guys you work with treating you right?"

I knew what it was like to be the youngest in a group of men. It usually went one of two ways. Either they were protective of you and took you under their wing or they were complete assholes. I was really hoping that Asher wasn't getting the second option.

"The ranch has been amazing. It's hard work and I tend to be sore by the end of the day, but the guys have all been awesome. They are showing me everything that I need to learn and they have been teaching me how to ride a horse. They are all really great, you don't have to worry about me."

"I'm always going to worry about you, but I am happy to hear that you are liking it so far and the guys are treating you right. Do you feel like you made the right decision?"

I knew it was easy at eighteen to think that the job you were choosing was going to be your career. There was that honeymoon period where everything felt great and exciting before reality hit you and you realized that that was going to be your life every single day for the next fifty years. I had been lucky that my honeymoon period hadn't ended with me feeling like I made a huge mistake and I was hoping that Asher and Greyson felt the same. As terrified as I was that Greyson would be in the army, I wanted him to feel like he had made the right decision. I wanted them both to find a career that they were in love with. A career that didn't feel like they were going to work every day, like I had been lucky enough to have.

"Completely. I mean, I'm sore as shit,

but soon that won't be an issue as my muscles get used to the work. I like being here. I like being around other guys who aren't geniuses. Guys who are good people and want to help animals. And these horses, oh man, they are the sweetest animals I have ever been around. Some of them have been abused and you can actually see their ribs. It's terrible and sad. But then when you start to earn their trust, it makes you feel this warmth and all of the effort and hours that go into building that trust is worth it."

I couldn't help but smile at hearing how much he was loving his job and it wasn't just the words that he said, I could hear it in his voice. It was a good sign and it was sounding like he was in the right place.

"I'm really happy to hear that, Ash,

truly. It's a huge relief to hear that you are loving it there and feel like it's where you want to be. Have you heard from Grey?"

Asher gave a chuckle before he spoke. "Oh yeah, he texts me all day long, mostly emojis of someone dying."

"So, it's not going well for him?" That was my biggest concern with Greyson. I knew he could handle anything in a classroom, but the military cared more about your physical health and strength over anything else, especially in Basic Training. It was going to be a lot on his body for those first six weeks until he graduated and then could move onto more specific training to be a medic.

"He's holding on. I did a lot of training with him beforehand so he's able to keep up. It's just a lot. The good news is that everyone is too exhausted by the end of the day to give him a hard time about any social cues he might have missed."

"I guess I should be thankful that you both have practice being the other. If nothing else, he could rely on how you act to get him through. Let me know though, if he tells you something bad happened. I don't want to be kept in the dark."

"I will, but you also can't go all papa bear and try to fix it either. He has to figure out how to be around normal people, you know that."

I did know that, but that didn't mean I was happy to accept it either. I was trying to remember that Xavier said that Greyson's unit would look out for him once he arrived in one. That they would make sure he was protected and help with any shortfalls in the social aspect of his personality. He just needed to make it through Basic Training and for Greyson's sake, I was hoping he would.

"I know. I just don't want to be blindsided. The same for you. I want to know if something happens, good or bad. You are both eighteen now, adults, and you don't need me to be your father anymore. Now I can be just your big brother and I don't want to lose the connection that we all have." Which was one of my greatest fears. Losing the special connection that the three of us shared. I had relied on it for so many years and I couldn't imagine not having it in my life.

"You're never going to lose that connection with us, Gage. We're always going to need you, no matter how old we are. I know this is hard on all of us, but especially you. So much of your life has been dedicated to taking care of us and making sure we had everything we needed, even going without just so we didn't have to. Our situation is new and it's scary, but we can all adapt to it and we can keep our connection to each other. And now when we do get to see each other, it will be even more special."

Fuck, leave it to Asher to go and say something deep and profound.

That was exactly what I meant when I told people that Asher was good with people. He knew what to say to them to help ease their worries. In a lot of ways, he was the voice of reason in my life and I was really going to miss having that.

"Well, now that you are going to make me cry, I'm going to let you go. You sound exhausted and you need proper sleep so you don't get hurt. I love you."

"I love you too. I'll let Grey know to call you when I talk with him tomorrow."

"Yes, please. I don't care when he calls me, I'll answer."

"I'll let him know. Be safe."

"You too. No standing behind a horse, I paid a lot of money for your teeth."

For both of their teeth. They both had to have braces from the age of twelve until seventeen. In hindsight, it was my fault they both needed it. They both sucked their thumbs when they were little in order to fall asleep, but they didn't stop until they were eight. The act of sucking their thumb after all of their teeth came in and even some of their adult teeth in the front had caused them to push back into their mouth. The result was two sets of braces and many dentist appointments. It was all worth it though, because now they both had perfect smiles and that helped a lot with Greyson's confidence.

"Worth every penny though," Asher teased.

"Yes, they were, but if you get them kicked out of your mouth, you will discover just how expensive teeth are."

"I promise not to stand behind a horse. Now, I gotta get some sleep. I love you, brother."

"Love you too. Good night."

"Night," he said, before he ended the call.

I felt a lot better now that I had gotten to speak to one of my brothers and I got an update on Greyson. I was hoping that I would be able to speak with him tomorrow at some point and I could hear for myself that he was doing okay and still feeling like he made the right decision.

With that stress and worry off of my mind, I turned my attention back to the reason that I had come out tonight and made my way back inside the bar. It was pretty busy for a Thursday night, but apparently it was Thirsty Thursday so the drinks were cheaper. That was fine by me, because I hated spending a lot of money on liquor.

I wasn't much of a drinker, but I figured that was connected to the twins. It was hard to be drunk at night when I might have to take care of them. I was always overly aware how easily things could take a bad turn. They could get sick or hurt and I needed to be able to care for them or, in the worst-case scenario, be sober so I could drive them to a hospital. Now that I was technically free to go crazy, I didn't have any interest in it. I think that was why I got along so well with some of the older guys at work. I didn't hold any interest in partying and making reckless mistakes. Though, they would argue that my motorcycle and love for skydiving was reckless and worse than a few drunken nights.

I made my way over to the bar to grab a beer. Afterward, I scanned the bar to see where all of the guys were. They were pretty spread out, some were playing pool or darts, others were talking with various women. I felt my heart beat faster as my gaze landed on the one person I never thought would be there.

Xavier.

Fuck, he looked good. He was wearing black, straight-cut jeans, with a black t-shirt underneath his black leather jacket that was unzipped. The man was sex on a stick and I hated that my entire body wanted him. It was insane, because I knew we would never work. It should have been clear cut, and yet my body was craving to feel him against it again. I didn't understand what it was about him, because I had been attracted to other tops before. I'd fooled around with other tops in the past and I had never had a problem walking away from them.

What the fuck made Xavier so different?

Xavier's eyes locked onto mine and once again I felt a wave of heat overtake my entire body. Everything in me wanted him and I could see the desire burning in his eyes too.

Our one time in the cave was not enough for either of us and I knew it was affecting him as well. I could see it in the way he avoided eye contact with me during class. The distance he placed between us, almost as if he was worried about being unable to resist touching me if we were close enough.

I couldn't resist giving him a sexy smirk and that seemed to trigger him. He made his way over toward me and my gaze couldn't help but travel down his body to his noticeable bulge. I didn't get to see his cock yet in some form of light, but I could remember clearly how impressive it felt. I would have loved to see it, to get to taste him.

"I'm surprised to see you here," I commented once he was close enough.

He leaned his arms against the bar top as he spoke, keeping his gaze on me. "Old people need a drink every once in a while."

The richness to his voice told me he'd already had a couple. Not that I could blame him, it had been a pretty shitty week so far.

"Isn't it past your bedtime?" I teased as I moved closer.

Fuck, this man was like a magnet.

"I don't know; you looking to tuck me in?" he countered with quite possibly the sexiest smirk I had ever seen.

"I could be persuaded into it." I ran my gaze up and down his body, lingering on his glorious ass. It really was a shame that he didn't bottom, because I had a feeling his ass would feel amazingly tight around my cock.

"I can think of something else I would rather persuade you into doing." He took a drink from his beer before he continued.

"You should walk me to my truck out back."

"You shouldn't be driving and I'm already buzzed." I wasn't too certain if he was planning on driving somewhere with me, but I couldn't let him drive with him being this buzzed.

"Who said anything about driving?" he countered before he moved back and started to head toward the back door. The logical part of my brain was telling me this was a bad idea, but the buzzed part of my brain was much louder.

I took a quick drink from my beer before I followed behind him. We headed out into the back parking lot and I saw that his truck was parked in the back, furthest away from the back door to the bar. It was also away from any overhanging lights.

I caught up to Xavier as he unlocked his truck and opened his back door. Without any hesitation, I hopped inside and was surprised at how clean it was. It was a really nice truck with soft leather seats.

The second he closed the door my mouth was on his. He hungrily kissed me back, instantly slipping his tongue into my mouth. Our tongues fought for control and dominance, neither one of us wanted to submit and it should have annoyed me, but it only turned me on even more.

My hands went to his coat and I started to pull it off. I needed to feel him, all of him. He followed my lead and we started to quickly divested each other of our clothes, only breaking the kiss long enough to rid each other of our shirts. He let out a deep moan as I took his bottom lip between my teeth.

"Fuck, I need to taste you," I moaned as I pulled back from him.

He ran his hand through my hair and gripped it slightly as he spoke in quite possibly the sexiest voice I had ever heard. "Then get your mouth on my cock."

He pushed my head down and I didn't resist. I was normally always in charge, but right now my whole body was tingling with need. It was dark, but there was enough light from the evening sky that I was able to just make out his cock and it did not disappoint. It was long and thick and it was already dripping with precum making it look very juicy.

I ran my tongue along his tip and moaned at the delicious taste that exploded along my tongue. I was instantly taking him within my mouth and he continued to push my head down until his tip hit the back of my throat. It wasn't enough for me though, because I was only getting half of him in my mouth. I relaxed my throat and continued to take him all the way down to his base and I was pleasantly rewarded with a deep moan from him. It was pretty clear that he wasn't used to being with a guy that could deep throat his cock.

"Fuck, you look so sexy with my cock down your throat and your ass up in the air."

I couldn't contain the moan of appreciation as he lightly thrust up and started to fuck my mouth. Usually I was always in control, in every aspect, but for some reason right now I wanted nothing more than for him to fuck the hell out of my mouth. I wanted my throat to be a bit sore come the morning. I couldn't stop moaning and whimpering at the feel of his cock sliding along my tongue and down my throat. My own cock was rock hard and I could feel my precum dripping down my tip. For the first time in my life, I thought I might come without even being touched.

I could feel his need building as his cock hardened and his thrusts became more erratic. He was getting close and I was in desperate need to feel him pulsing within my throat. To feel his cum running down it. I already knew he was going to taste amazing and my mouth was watering just at the very thought of it.

With a final snap of his hips, Xavier gave a hiss followed by a long groan as his cock pulsed and his cum shot down my throat. I gratefully swallowed every last drop that he had for me. His taste did not disappoint and I knew if I wasn't careful, I could become addicted to it, which wouldn't go well for me considering I was leaving after this course.

Xavier grasped my hair and pulled my head up off his cock and immediately was capturing my mouth with his own. His hand left my hair and both of his hands went to the back of my thighs and before I even had a chance to register what he was doing, he was flipping us so my back was on the seat and he was laying on top of me. His hand traveled up my thigh to my ass as I pressed my knees against his hips. I could hear him rummaging around for something, but I was too focused on his lips against mine, on the closeness of his half-hard cock to my own pulsing one.

Far too soon for my liking, he was breaking the kiss and he spoke as he started to kiss along my neck.

"Trust me."

I had no idea what he was asking me to trust him on, but right now my mind could barely function and everything felt way too good to even care enough to figure it out. All I knew was that he was kissing his way down my chest, toward my cock and that was the only thing that I needed to know.

The second he reached my cock, he didn't even waste a single second before he was taking me into his mouth and quickly moving down to my base, something I knew wasn't an easy task given my large size. The sudden heat that engulfed my cock had my back arching, pushing my cock just a bit further down his throat. I couldn't stop moaning at the sensation of his mouth as it moved over my hardness.

I briefly struggled with where to put my hands. Normally, I would have my fingers tangled in the guy's hair and I would be controlling them, but I knew that wasn't something Xavier was going to be content with. Given no other choice, I raised my hands above my head and gripped the door handle.

Xavier's mouth worked my cock like he was born to do it. I was so consumed, so lost in the pleasure that was coursing through my body that I didn't even notice that Xavier had ulterior motives until his lubed up middle finger was pushing past the muscles of my very virgin hole.

I blinked my eyes open and looked down to see Xavier looking right back at me as he continued to suck my cock and slowly push his finger inside of me. Every intention of telling him to stop, to ask what the fuck he thought he was doing, completely died on my tips at just the sight of his mouth wrapped around my cock. I couldn't do anything but moan and whimper as I watched my dick disappear down his throat over and over.

Suddenly, the foreign finger inside of me became unimportant. I had to admit, it felt odd, but it didn't bother me as much as I thought it would. Though that could just be because Xavier's experienced mouth was devouring my cock at the same time.

What I couldn't understand before was why my partners loved being a bottom; it didn't feel overly good to me. All of that went right out the window when Xavier's finger hit something inside of me and my involuntary sharp cry echoed off of the walls of Xavier's truck. I quickly followed that with a whimper as Xavier removed his glorious mouth from my cock. He started to kiss up my stomach once again as he spoke.

"That's the sweet spot. That spot that sends electric pleasure waves all throughout your body. You've hit it in other people, I'm sure, but you've never felt it before. Not until me."

He started to rub a circle all over my sweet spot and I couldn't contain the repeated deep moans that escaped my body. I had never felt that kind of pleasure before and if that was what I made all of my partners feel like, then I completely understood why they loved sex so much.

Xavier leaned down even closer, his lips almost touching mine as he moved his finger even faster inside of me.

"Feels good, doesn't it, baby? Imagine just how good it would feel to have my cock sliding back and forth over it."

The sound that came out of my mouth couldn't have come from me. It was a mixture of a mewl and a whine. It was needy and not something I would ever associate myself with. I couldn't help it though. My whole body was being consumed with pleasure. Xavier was taking me to new heights, heights I had never thought would even be possible. My need to come was growing too great.

"Please, I need to come. Please," I begged, panting even harder as Xavier picked up his pace once again.

"Begging already, now you really are

sounding like a bottom. Whose bottom are you?"

"Yours," I quickly caved. "Please."

"You're so close. You're gonna come any second now. I can feel your walls tightening. I'm going to make you come without touching your cock. I'm going to milk you for every last drop."

My mind was spinning and I felt completely out of control. Not a normal feeling for me but one I wondered now if might just be able to get used to. I couldn't stop moaning and panting. My whole body was tingling and my legs were trembling from my need to come. None of that had ever happened to me before and I thought if I knew that it was possible, I would have tried it a hell of a lot earlier.

I didn't know what it was about Xavier that made it so easy for me to submit to him. I had been with other tops before and if any of them had tried something like that, I doubt I would have let them. And yet there I was whining and begging Xavier for more. It was like he had this power over me and instead of being scared over it, my whole body was loving it.

A sudden heat exploded within my stomach and quickly traveled all over my body. My cock pulsed and my whole body went rigid as my walls clamped around his digit and I was finally pushed over that cliff. An extensive, deep moan filled the truck as I squeezed the door handle with every ounce of strength that I had within me. The orgasm was unlike anything I had ever felt before. I wasn't shooting out cum, but rather it was running out of me and it kept me at my peak the whole time. Every time Xavier's finger went over my sweet spot, more cum would come out. I was completely powerless under his hand. All I could do was moan and writhe at the pleasure that was scorching through me.

"That's it, come for me, baby," Xavier said as he started to kiss down my chest once more.

I felt his tongue licking up my cum and every couple of licks he would run it over my still leaking tip, sending electric shock waves down my cock. I was in a complete fog. I couldn't function. I could barely breathe. All I could do was pant and ride out the longest orgasm I had ever had in my life. I don't even know how long it went on for before I felt Xavier's finger slipping from my hole and I couldn't stop the whimper at the sudden loss of him inside of me.

I shouldn't have wanted him to have any part of himself inside of me and yet now I couldn't help but wonder what it would have felt like to have his cock buried deep inside of me. I was so lightheaded and even my teeth felt like they were tingling. I knew that was just from the lack of oxygen, but holy fuck.

"I told you I would make you feel good."

I didn't even have to look at him to know that he was smirking, the fucking asshole. And had I been able to have the brain function to form those words, I would have said them. Instead, all that came out of me was a breathy groan, which he promptly chuckled at.

"I'll call you a cab while you try and get your brain to work. You're gonna need your rest for tomorrow."

I knew he was right. I had another long day in class and I was going to need to be awake for it. At the same time, the thought of moving was really unappealing, let alone having to get dressed in the back of his truck. I had to do it, I knew that, but not just yet. I just needed a few more minutes to come back down from the best orgasm I had ever fucking had in my life.

Part of me couldn't help but wonder though, what would happen between us now?

Would this just be a one-time thing again, like the cave, or would it become a more regular occurrence?

I didn't dare vocalize my question for one very simple reason, I was too afraid of what his answer would be. And more disturbingly, I was too afraid of what my reaction to his answer would be. Those were emotions that I didn't need to unpack right now. Right now, all I had to do was keep breathing so I could eventually manage to get dressed. That was all that mattered tonight.

CHAPTER SIXTEEN

Xavier

IT WAS FINALLY Friday and class was wrapped up.

I had managed to make it through without pushing Gage up against a wall and kissing him, a personal achievement that at times, I wasn't certain I would actually achieve today. I didn't know what it was about him, but I couldn't stop thinking about him and how fucking amazing his body felt against mine.

I knew we shouldn't have done anything last night, especially not in my truck where someone could have seen us. We had both been drinking, me more than him, and I knew it would be a terrible idea, but my body wanted his and it wasn't taking no for an answer. Now, I had no idea what was going to happen between us.

I knew what Jackson would say, to go for it and just enjoy the meaningless fling. I knew logically that would be the best course of action, but part of me didn't want a meaningless fling with Gage. There was something special about him, maybe it was because he was young and had sacrificed having a proper childhood to raise his twin brothers. Maybe it was because he was genuinely a good person and wanted to do what he could to help people and be the best role model that he could be for his brothers. He was different and not like anyone I had ever met or interacted with before.

My head was so screwed up over this, but I had to push Gage aside, at least for now. Tonight, I had a different battle to forge through.

I pulled my truck up to the street parking for the basketball court. I knew every Friday night after school Dexter would come here to shoot some hoops first before heading home for dinner. He hadn't returned my calls and I had decided to be more proactive. I couldn't leave it up to him to see me any longer. I would respect his space, but I couldn't go any longer not speaking to my son, not knowing him. I knew I had screwed up plenty of times when he was younger, but I was human and it was time that he saw me as such. It was going to take work, but I was no stranger to hard work or for a challenge that everyone said I would never be able to succeed with. I had gone off to war and faced the worst that humanity had to offer, speaking with Dexter and getting back into his life was going to be easy compared to all of that shit.

I glanced over at the basketball court and saw that Dexter was there alone just shooting some hoops. The basketball court was in really good shape thanks to the very high-end neighborhood that Dexter and Kate lived in.

Kate had remarried a handful of years ago now, to a doctor, and she had finally achieved the life she always wanted, the life that a military man couldn't ever give her.

Even from my spot in the truck I could see that my son was tall. He was a decent size as well, he had clearly been working out. I had no idea how well this was going to go over, but I was hoping that when I left this conversation it would be in a better position than when it started. I wasn't going to get anywhere if I never got out of my truck though.

Letting out a long slow breath from my nose to try and calm my nerves down, I climbed out of my truck and made my way across the street. I was relieved that he was alone, because the last thing I wanted was to make him feel embarrassed in front of his friends. I also didn't really want an audience for the rejection I was confident would be coming my way.

"Dex," I called out shakily as I walked onto the basketball court.

At the sound of my voice, his body stiffened, he stopped dribbling and the ball bounced off. He was clearly not expecting for me to be there or quite possibly to ever hear my voice in person again. His back was to me and I was praying that he would at least turn around. Very slowly he did turn around and I was finally able to lay eyes directly on my son for the first time in years. Seeing his face so clearly, it felt like I was being punched in the gut. He looked so much like me when I was his age.

My hands itched to be able to reach out and touch him, to pull him in for a hug and just feel him against me again. I didn't dare move though, too scared that it would snap Dexter out of his shock and he would dismiss me.

"What are you doing here?" Dexter asked, with a hard voice. No *Dad*, no *hello*, just straight to the point. I guess I shouldn't have been too surprised, that was how I always acted when I didn't want to have to interact with someone.

"I came here to see you. You don't ever answer your phone when I call and you never call me back. I wanted to see you. I wanted to make sure you were okay and be in your life. You're my son, Dex."

I didn't even know how to start the conversation. I didn't know how to word how I felt or what my expectations were. I was completely at his mercy and I could only imagine what his mother had been putting into his head. He was my son, but he was a stranger standing in front of me and I hated it. I hated every second of it.

"And? Being a parent isn't a right, it's a privilege. A privilege that you haven't seemed to care about all that much. I know you were there for the first six years of my life, but you haven't been there for me for the past eleven, almost twelve years."

"Your mother," I started, but he cut me off before I could even start to defend myself.

"No, you don't get to do that. You don't get to blame it all on mom. I know she isn't easy to deal with, to live with. I've lived with her every single day for the past seventeen years, you think I don't know that she has extreme beliefs? You think I like going to church three times a week?"

"Three? Shit, it used to be once," I

couldn't help but say. Kate had always been very involved with the church thanks to her parents, but I didn't know she had increased her involvement that much.

"Yeah, well, I guess when you find out that the man you have been in love with for the majority of your life is actually gay, it makes you go to extremes to be able to deal with it," he said with a small shrug, but there was no malice in his voice.

I was surprised that he knew I was gay and that was the reason for the divorce though. I had expected for Kate to make sure that never got out.

"You know?" I couldn't help but ask.

"Since I was twelve. Mom didn't tell me, I overheard her and Dan talking about it one night. She was worried that I would turn out to be a deviant like you, hence all of the church. She doesn't know that I know, it's not a conversation that we've ever had. She prefers to pretend that you don't exist, which is pretty accurate."

I was shocked at how well this conversation was going. I knew it wasn't very warm and fuzzy, but I had expected for him to act his age, to yell at me and tell me to go fuck myself. Instead, he was being relatively calm and rational and it actually pissed me off. I had left a six-year-old boy who always wanted one more bedtime story. Who would stomp his feet and pout for hours if he didn't get what he wanted. And now, standing here before me was a young man, a soon-to-be adult who was levelheaded and well spoken.

I had missed those formidable years where he grew into the man that he was today and that pissed me off. I wasn't mad at him, I was mad at myself, because I shouldn't have allowed for things to get to this level. I should have put a stop to all of it years ago. I wanted to ask him if he was gay as well, but that would have been too personal and honestly, I hadn't earned that level of honesty from him.

"Things were not black and white back then, Dex. I tried to fight for custody of you, but my job made it impossible to get joint custody. The judge left all of the visitations to your mother and she did everything she could to keep me from you. If I could go back in time I would change everything. I would have changed my career so I could be home more and have had a chance at joint custody. I made a lot of mistakes where you were concerned and I have to live with those regrets. I know it will take work, I have a lot to make up for, but I just want the chance to be in your life now. You are my son and I love you."

All I could do was lay everything down on the line and hope that he would be open-minded enough to try to form a relationship with me. I knew it wouldn't be as strong or as deep as it would have been had I been there for him growing up. But that didn't mean we couldn't have something real, something stable with each other.

"I know things with mom weren't easy. I know you tried. I found all of the court documents in the attic. That's not why I won't call you back. It has nothing to do with mom and everything to do with you."

I took a few steps closer to him as I spoke in a calm voice. "What about me?

What is it that is keeping you from calling me back?"

"Come on, Dad, you really don't know?" he asked with a shake of his head.

The problem was, I didn't know. I didn't know what it was that I had done that was preventing my own son from reaching out to me. I didn't think I had done anything wrong that would warrant him not wanting to ever speak with me. The voicemails were polite and welcoming, I thought. I had never demanded to know why he wouldn't talk with me. I had never gotten angry or threatened him in any way. I had always left the ball in his court, despite how difficult it was for me to do that. I had no idea what the problem could be.

"No, I really don't know. I don't think

I've done anything wrong with reaching out to you," I said, not even bothering with trying to hide my confusion.

"Almost every time you call and leave a voicemail you're drunk. Only one out of ten phone calls will you be sober. I don't want to talk to you if you are going to be drunk all the time." I went to speak, but he held his hand up and stopped me as he continued. "I'm not judging. I know you were in the Air Force. I looked up your unit online, so I know the type of places you were sent to, the things you would have seen. I understand why you would struggle, but I can't handle your problems on top of my own and mom's. I know that doesn't sound fair, but I have to deal with mom and her insane rules and her fucked up head. On top of that, I have to try and deal with my own anxiety and mental health problems. I can't handle anyone else's demons. I'm sorry, but I can't."

The deep hurt and pain radiated throughout his voice and it instantly sent a wave of pain through my chest to hear. I hated that he was hurting and I didn't even know why. That he was having his own mental health problems and I didn't even know what they were. I should have been there for him. I should have been someone that he could call when he was having trouble, and instead I was someone that he couldn't call because he couldn't handle more than what was already on his plate. I knew there had been times that I had called him drunk, but I didn't think I sounded drunk. I didn't think he would have an issue over it. That was my fault though, because I should have thought more deeply about it.

"Dex, I'm so sorry. You never should have to deal with any problem that either of your parents have. I didn't realize that I had called you that many times when I was intoxicated. It wasn't fair to you and it won't happen again. I want to be there for you. I want to help you with whatever you are going through. I'm always going to be there for you."

I couldn't keep my hands to myself any longer. I reached out and placed my hands on his biceps and I could feel the slight tremble within his body. He was trying to hold in his own emotions, his own demons, and all I wanted was for him to let them go, to give them to me. I could take them on and then he would be free from them. Only I knew it didn't work that way. I couldn't take his demons from him; all I could do was be there to help him fight them. All he had to do was let me.

"Tell me what is going on. Let me help you," I practically begged. There was so much hurt within him, he couldn't carry it alone anymore.

"You can't. You don't get it, Dad, you can't help me because you can't even help yourself. You're getting drunk all week long just to deal with your own demons. You can't help me because you aren't healthy yourself. Mom can't help me for the exact same reason. I'm on my own with this," he said, tears starting to build in his eyes.

I felt like my heart was being ripped right out of my chest. I had failed him on so many levels and I couldn't keep failing him.

"No, you aren't alone. You don't have to deal with this on your own. I'm going to be there for you. I'm going to stop drinking and get help for my issues, so I can be stronger and be what you need to help you with your demons. You are my son, I love you, and there is nothing in this world that I wouldn't do for you," I said as I wiped the tear that rolled down his cheek with my thumb.

It was time that I got my head out of my ass and started to get healthy again. I didn't think I was causing anyone any pain with my actions. I'd thought I was only hurting myself, but that was me being blind and selfish. My actions were hurting my son and that wasn't something I was ever going to tolerate again. He needed me, he needed my help, and in order to be the man that he needed

I had to get healthy. I had to get my shit together so I could help him heal from whatever trauma that he had endured.

"I feel so alone in this world," Dexter admitted, and it only cut me deeper.

Fuck, how could I have screwed up so much?

"You aren't anymore, Son, I promise you." I pulled him in for a hug and he easily wrapped his arms around me. "I love you," I said, and I had to fight back my own tears. I was finally hugging my son; after eleven years I was hugging him.

This meeting had gone a lot differently than I had been expecting, but it was also good. I had one hell of a fight ahead of me, it wasn't going to be easy, but it was a battle I was going to be fighting to win with everything inside me. It wasn't just my life on the line this time around, but

Dexter's as well and I was not going to allow anything to happen to him. I didn't care what it took, I was going to be getting him healthy even if that meant I had to fix my fucked up head first. There was no war that I wouldn't go to if it meant protecting him. He was my whole world and I was never going to lose it again.

CHAPTER SEVENTEEN

Gage

WHEN I WOKE up this morning I was actually looking forward to class. So much so that I wasn't even bothered by the fact that it was Monday and typically Monday mornings sucked. None of that bothered me today though, because I was going to get to see Xavier.

I had no idea how he was going to

interact with me, if he would acknowledge me or ignore me like he did the last time we fooled around. So far, there hadn't been any time for either of us to interact with each other.

Once we got into the classroom, Jackson had immediately started on different word problems for various scenarios that could cause a forest fire and ways it could spread. We needed to determine the best course of action and how much time we would have before the fire spread given a wide degree of variables. The first few weren't too bad and we did the work together; however, now that we were working on our own the problems were increasing in difficulty level.

Now it was nearing the end of the day and I still had a few more scenarios to work through and everyone but one other cadet had completed their work and left. Jackson was currently helping the other cadet, leaving me on my own. I could have gone over there, but I hated feeling like an idiot, something that was left over from my high school days.

I knew I had missed a lot of school for a good reason, but that didn't make it any easier when I had to sit in class and not understand anything that was going on around me. To be the one kid who was confused when everyone else had long since got it. Teachers would always say there was no such thing as a stupid question, but I knew that was a lie, because when you had to ask for the same thing to be explained a dozen times, that question started to look pretty stupid.

I'd wanted to take this course so I could better my skills and be more useful in the future, but now it was looking like I was only going to fail, which meant returning home to the firehouse a failure.

The sound of a chair being pulled out drew my attention away from my paper to see Xavier had come over. I had been so lost in thought that I didn't even notice him coming back into the room or making his way toward me. He turned the chair around before he straddled it just to the left of me as he spoke. "You know there is nothing wrong with asking for help."

"You've clearly never been the kid who hides in the back of a classroom begging the universe for the ground to open up and swallow you whole." I tried to make it sound like I was joking, but I couldn't do it. My insecurities and disappointment in myself were coming through too much.

To my surprise, Xavier reached over and placed his hand over top of mine as he spoke. "You sacrificed a lot growing up for your brothers. Having to work to pay the bills and to take care of your dying mother, school would have been the lowest priority you had. The system failed you, Gage, not the other way around."

I wanted to believe him, I did, but sitting there and being one of the last people to leave was only making the voices in my head louder, repeatedly telling me I couldn't do this.

"The guys back at my firehouse think I took this course because I'm an adrenaline junky. And yeah, I do love to get my heart pumping. I skydive and bungee jump at least once a month, but that's not why I'm doing this. I just want to be useful. The more skills I can learn, then the more useful I can be to the department and the more people I can help. I knew there was going to be class work for this course, I just didn't expect for the material to be this hard. I don't think I'll be able to pass the final exam."

I hated that my insecurities were bubbling up, especially in front of Xavier. I was supposed to be strong and dominant, and yet here I was sounding every bit my age.

"You're not going to fail. I don't care if I have to tutor you every night and on the weekends, you are going to pass this course. Out of all of the guys here, you are the only one who is doing this for good reasons. You're not doing it to show off or to brag to some guy in a bar. You genuinely want to help people and that is something worth fighting for. You can do this. I believe in you."

The pure strength in his voice had an instant calming effect on my nerves. I wasn't doing this alone and that reality hit me like a ton of bricks. I had spent so much of my life having to handle things on my own. Having to be the strong one, the one who could handle anything, the one who never complained.

I hadn't really had anyone that I could rely on, not since my mom got sick. Xavier's offer of support left me with mixed feelings, because as desperate as I was to have someone in my corner, someone who I could be vulnerable with, I also knew that it wouldn't last. Sooner than I would like, I would be leaving and going back home and Xavier would be here. I would have to go back to being on my own, even more so now that the twins were both gone. Allowing myself to rely on Xavier's strength here could devastate me for when I returned home.

Picking up on my inability to speak, Xavier thankfully changed the subject. "We'll take it one step at a time, it'll get easier the more you do."

I highly doubted it was ever going to get easier, but I appreciated the offer.

CHAPTER EIGHTEEN

Gage

THREE HOURS. THREE of the longest hours of my fucking life, but the worksheet was finally done. I wasn't too certain that the questions had gotten easier, but I had managed to get through them and I suppose that was the best I could hope for.

I did enjoy spending the past three

hours sitting next to Xavier and getting to be close to him. I was struggling with not leaning over and just kissing him, even after Jackson and the other cadet left two hours ago. I had never felt this level of attraction to someone before, not even when I had discovered that I was gay and this whole world opened up to me.

The whole weekend I couldn't stop thinking about him and about our time in his back seat. I'd spent most of the weekend trying to keep my cock from getting hard and even that I wasn't successful at. I had jerked off six times in the past two days. I didn't masturbate that much when puberty hit, for fuck's sake.

It was like something had awoken within me, which made no sense because I had been having sex since I was sixteen, for close to nine years now. I was a top, I knew I was a top, I had loved being a top and not once in those nine years had I ever thought about being a bottom. And all it took was one fucking time in the back seat of Xavier's truck to make me question everything. What added to my confusion, I had thought about what it might be like to have another guy touch me like that, to be submissive to another man, but I couldn't do it. It left me feeling uninterested and unsatisfied. It was only when I thought about Xavier did it have any positive affect on me. It made no sense, but at that point I was just over trying to understand it. All I needed to know was that it felt good and I wanted more. I didn't have to over-analyze it to death.

"Thank you for staying here and

helping me," I said, flashing him a genuine smile as I started to pack up.

"It's fine. With some more practice, you'll be able to do them easily. I know Jackson and I are on everyone's ass to be able to do all of this work, but the reality is once you are working on a team there is always someone that does something better and you naturally allow them to handle that stuff. You mostly need to know how to do this as a precaution in case you end up somewhere alone."

That was comforting and I knew from being at my own firehouse that lots of people had specialties and you rely on them within the field. Not everyone could be an expert at everything.

I was getting concerned about Xavier right then though. His hands were shaking, progressively getting worse as the minutes ticked by. He was starting to become pale and he just looked like he was getting sick. Xavier stood from his chair, but he leaned and I was just able to grab his arm to keep him steady.

"Hey, you okay?" I couldn't keep the concern from my voice. He really wasn't looking too good.

"Yeah, just coming down with a bug. I'll see you tomorrow." He went to move away, but I was not going to let him get away that easily. He was trembling and shaky on his feet. There was no way in hell that I was going to let him drive himself anywhere.

"Slow down, hot stuff, there's no way you can drive like this. Come on, I'll drive you home."

"I'll be fine," Xavier protested and I might have taken it seriously had he not sound like complete shit right now.

"No, you're sick and you are in no condition to be driving. Don't argue with me on this." I wasn't going to tolerate his macho bullshit. He was clearly not in any shape to drive and would be a hazard on the road.

I kept my hand on his arm to make sure he didn't collapse as we headed out of the station and toward his truck. He reluctantly passed me the keys before I helped him get into the passenger seat.

I tossed my bag into the back seat before jumping into the driver's side. My mind was instantly conjuring up what we had done in this truck just forty-eight hours prior and my body was immediately responding, but none of that was going to be taking place right now. A quick glance over at Xavier told me that he was not doing well at all.

After getting his address, I punched it into the GPS so he wouldn't have to give me directions and we headed out. I didn't talk on the drive, I knew personally that when I didn't feel well the last thing I wanted to do was answer all sorts of questions or have to hold up on my end of a conversation. Based on how pale he was looking, he was definitely having a personal battle with his stomach and talking meant a greater chance of throwing up.

Once we arrived at his address, I parked in the first spot I found on the street. I had to admit that it wasn't the area I had been expecting. There wasn't really a gang or ghetto area in the city, but this was as close as you were going to get to one. Which was surprising that he was living here because I knew he made more than enough money for a decent place. I climbed out of the truck and went around to his side as he started to get out. The trembling was overtaking his whole body at this point though, and he could barely walk. I tossed his arm over my shoulders as I spoke.

"I got you. Come on, let's get you up. What number is your apartment?" I was really hoping he was going to tell me it was on the first floor.

"Three-ten. It's on the third floor," he said with a tight voice and I could tell it was taking everything in him to not throw up right that minute, which I appreciated.

Of course though, his apartment was on the third floor and with how old these buildings looked, I knew there was no chance in hell there was an elevator. And even if there was one, I doubted that was a place you wanted to be in.

We worked together, getting into the apartment building and going up the stairs. It was not easy by any stretch of the imagination, but we finally made it to his apartment.

I took the keys from his shaky hands and quickly unlocked his front door before we stumbled inside. I didn't spend much time looking around, because I knew he needed the bathroom before his will power failed us both. I quickly took him to the right and down the very short hallway to the bathroom. I brought him in and helped to sit him down on the floor right next to the toilet.

"Let's get this off real quick," I said, as I bent down and started to remove his jacket. It was more comfortable to throw up without a leather jacket on, and, yup, knew that from personal experience. With his jacket off, I then turned my attention to his black boots.

"I got it," Xavier's shaky voice filled the silence of the bathroom.

"You can barely function while shaking so badly. Just relax. Do you need anything? Water, a pillow or a blanket?" I had no idea how long he was going to be stuck in the bathroom and I knew from experience that sometimes it was nice to just curl up and try to sleep it off on the cool bathroom floor. I knew some would find that gross, but when you were constantly fighting with throwing up, it was also nice knowing that if you did need to puke, you only had a few inches to reach the toilet and not twenty feet.

"No, I'll be fine. Just hit the lock on the

front door on your way out."

"All right, call me if you need anything though. And thank you for your help tonight," I said, flashing him a warm smile as I grabbed his boots and his jacket to bring out into the living area.

"Thanks for driving me."

"I hope you feel better soon," I said before I headed out, closing the bathroom door behind me.

I brought his items out into the living area and for the first time I was able to see what his place looked like. I placed his boots down by the front door and draped his jacket over the back of a chair. It certainly wasn't what I had been expecting for his place. It was a bachelor apartment, one that was not very clean or organized. There was nothing personal in the whole place, nothing on his walls, nothing that would indicate who Xavier was. There was a bed that was on a box spring on the floor and the sheets were a mess. There were take out containers on an old coffee table and spread over the kitchen counter. There were empty liquor bottles and a huge pile of empty beer cans to go with it. A quick look in his small fridge and cupboards showed me that there wasn't any food in this place. Now it was all making sense. Xavier didn't have a stomach bug. He was going through alcohol withdrawals.

Fuck.

That was a completely different level of seriousness. I had once helped a fellow firefighter going through alcohol withdrawals and they were horrible on his body. For the first week it was the worst and then it would get easier during that second week. Even after the withdrawals, you had to deal with the reasons behind the drinking.

For Xavier, that meant him having to deal with his trauma from going to war. It wouldn't be surprising for him to have PTSD. Most veterans returned home with it and Xavier was functioning, but it appeared that he had been functioning with alcohol. For some reason though, he was trying to quit, and I couldn't help but wonder why. Regardless of the reason, he was trying to stop and I wasn't about to leave and let him go through this alone.

I removed my coat and started by making the bed. I'd get out here cleaned up before I would go and check in on Xavier. He didn't have to go through this alone and he was going to need all of the help that he could get until the withdrawals were over. I was just hoping that Xavier would be able to hold on and fight long enough to make it through the withdrawals and then he could start to work on healing from the trauma.

CHAPTER NINETEEN

Xavier

I WAS DYING.

That was the only way I could think of to describe what I was feeling. It felt like my insides were trying to escape my body. Every time I threw up, I kept waiting to see if my kidney would be in the toilet. I knew withdrawals were going to be bad. I had done the research so I was mentally prepared for what was to come, but I didn't expect for it to feel as bad as it did.

I couldn't stop shaking, my stomach was cramping, I was throwing up things I had eaten when I was twelve at this point. I was freezing, but sweating at the same time, and my skin felt like there were millions of bugs crawling underneath it. I felt like complete shit and I knew it was only going to get worse as each day passed for the next week. I had been through a lot in my life, but detoxing was looking like it would be the hardest thing I had ever gone through and that included my time overseas.

If I was just doing this for myself, I would have said fuck it. I wouldn't be going through it. I wouldn't be putting my body through this torture. But I wasn't doing this just for me.

GAGE

I was doing it for Dexter.

He needed a parent. He needed someone who could be strong for him so he had the freedom to work through whatever trauma he was holding on to. He needed me to be healthy and I wasn't going to let him down.

Not ever again.

I was curled up into a ball of misery on the cool bathroom floor when the sound of my front door closing caught my attention. I should have been alone. Gage should have left long ago, and considering he was the only other person who knew I lived here, that meant a stranger was in my home. It would be just my luck to be getting robbed right now, though I didn't know what they'd think I had that would be worth stealing. I didn't own shit.

I opened my eyes when I heard

footsteps coming toward me. To my surprise though, it wasn't a burglar, but Gage. He had left earlier, I knew he did because I heard the door close, but for some reason he was back.

"What are you doing here?" I managed to get out, but it was a struggle with my stomach.

He had removed his coat and he was standing there with one of my pillows and a blue Gatorade in his hands. He approached me as he spoke. "Here, putting your head elevated, even a bit, will help with any lightheadedness or dizziness. I also got you some Gatorades to help get some electrolytes into you. I know you are just going to throw it up, but some will still be absorbed through your stomach and that can help reduce the nausea."

I let him help me raise my head just enough for him to get the pillow underneath it. What I couldn't figure out was why he had come back. I wasn't his responsibility. He had class in the morning. He should have been back at the dorms getting a proper sleep. He was going to need his brain fresh to survive the class work. I'd meant what I said; I would tutor him and make sure he was able to pass the written exam. Gage had heart and the desire to help people, and that was worth the time and effort I would have to put in so he would be able to pass the exam.

"What are you doing here?" I asked again, because he clearly ignored my question last time.

"I know you don't have the flu. Alcohol withdrawals are serious and you shouldn't have to be going through them alone. I've done this before with one of the guys at my firehouse. I'm not an expert, but I at least know a few tricks. I got rid of your empties as well, by the way, and I double-checked that there wasn't any left in the apartment. I also cleaned up a bit."

"OCD?" I teased, that was easier than me having to face my feelings about someone being here and actually helping me. I was used to doing everything on my own ever since my parents died. I didn't exactly know how to handle Gage's willingness to help without me even asking for it.

He gave me a rich smile as he spoke. "No, not even close. I'm just used to cleaning. Between the twins when they were younger and my mom being sick, taking care of people is something I am really good at."

He got up and grabbed a washcloth from my bathroom stand before he wet it and rang it out. It only made sense that Gage would be a natural when it came to care giving. He did have a lot of experience with it and I had to imagine while his mother was going to radiation and chemotherapy that she was sick often.

I had a lot of respect for the woman. To be told that she was going to die no matter what treatment was done, but to still go through it. To put herself through that pain and added sickness just so she could get a couple more years on this Earth. And not for herself, she did it for her children, so Gage could get to a legal age where her children could stay together. It was one of the more honorable and courageous things I had ever heard.

Gage bent back down and he placed the cool, damp cloth against my forehead as he spoke. "This can help settle your stomach. Something about the cold against your body that kinda calms everything down."

"Thank you, but you don't have to stay. I'll be okay. You need to sleep for class tomorrow." I could admit that I was not very good at having people around me when I was sick and vulnerable. It had been like that my whole life and after the Air Force it did get worse. I was miserable, but that didn't mean I needed to make others miserable around me. Gage should be back at the dorms, sleeping and focusing on the course. He didn't need to worry about me.

He went and shuffled over so his back

was against the wall and he was sitting with his legs stretched out in front of him by my head as he spoke. "This is far from my first all-nighter and it won't be my last. The first day is always the hardest and I know I have to go to class come morning, but the least I can do is be here for you during the first part of the twenty-four hours from hell. I'm not leaving, so you might as well accept it. It's not exactly like you can strong-arm me out of here. You might as well use me as a distraction.

I could keep arguing, but it wasn't going to do me any good. He wasn't going to leave me alone and if I was honest with myself, I didn't want him to. I closed my eyes as I spoke. "Can you text Jackson from my phone and tell him I won't be in? Just tell him I have the flu. He'll know it's bullshit, but he won't call me out on it."

Another reason why I loved that man, he was perfectly fine to leave you in our own ignorant bubble.

"Got it," Gage said as he reached for my phone that I had placed on the counter by the sink. "Can I ask why the sudden desire to quit drinking?"

The first thought that came to my mind was that it was none of his fucking business. However, if he was going to be here for me and help me get through the withdrawals, he deserved to know my reasoning behind it. He deserved to know what I was fighting for so if there did come a point where I wanted to give in, he would be able to remind me.

"Friday night I went and saw Dex. It had been years since we'd talked. My ex-wife didn't handle it very well when she discovered I was gay. She comes from a highly religious family and she saw it as a sign from the devil. She took Dex and I had to fight to try and see him. I went through the court process, but I was in the Air Force and my job came with an unstable schedule. The judge didn't grant me joint custody and left visitation rights up to her. I almost never got to see him and as he got older, Dex started to grow distant with me, angry with me. He wouldn't take my calls, wouldn't return them. He didn't want to see me."

"I'm sorry, that couldn't have been easy. I can't even imagine what I would have done had something like that happened with the twins," he said with complete understanding to his voice, and part of me knew that was why I was telling him any of this to begin with. He would understand where I was coming from. He would understand the pain that I had been going through.

"Friday night, I decided to just show up at the basketball court by his house. He likes to play and I knew he went there after school. I wanted to explain myself, to tell him that I was gay and that I had fought for him. He already knew though. This whole time I thought he didn't want to speak with me was because of the lies his mother was telling him. Turns out, he didn't want to speak with me because I called him when I was drunk more times than sober. He said he understood that I would have seen horrible shit overseas, but he had his own problems and struggles with mental health, he couldn't take mine on." It still hurt to know that my own son was struggling and he wouldn't tell me about it because he didn't think I was stable and healthy enough to help him. I knew I had been a shit father, but I didn't know that was the reason I had been.

Gage let out a low whistle before he spoke with concern in his tone. "That's deep and fucked up. Did he tell you about his struggles?"

"I asked, but he said I wasn't able to help him, because I couldn't help myself. I promised him that I would get healthy again, so I could be strong and stable, so I could be able to help him carry his problems. I think something happened to him, but he's not willing to talk about it with me. Not yet, at least. I have to get better for him, so I can help him get better. I started to wean myself off from the booze, but when I ran out last night, I couldn't bring myself to purchase more just so I could quit. I wasn't planning on doing this cold turkey, but maybe it's better to get it over and done with."

I wasn't really all that certain on what the best way to do it was, but I was in the thick of things now and I was not about to change course. I was going to quit cold turkey and just hope for the best at this point.

"It's not going to be easy. You are going to feel like shit for about a week, but then you will start to feel more human by the end of it. Quitting drinking is only one part of it though. You'll need to speak with a therapist to correct the trauma, otherwise you will slip right back into the bottle."

"I know and I will once I get through the withdrawals."

I hated the idea of speaking with a

shrink, but I also knew that I had to otherwise I wouldn't be able to get through the cravings once they started. I had to take this seriously if I was going to be able to help Dexter. He needed to see me working hard and doing things the right way in order for him to start as well. I was doing this for him and there wasn't anything I wouldn't do for my son. The first step was getting through these withdrawals then the real work would start.

CHAPTER TWENTY

Xavier

GUNFIRE WAS COMING at me from all directions. I was fighting to hold the chopper steady as I picked up the SEAL Team that were in desperate need of an exfil. The situation was a serious clusterfuck that was only getting worse as each second ticked by. Landing had been difficult, but we couldn't have them repel up with this much gunfire. They would just have been moving targets dangling in the air. The pings of bullets off of the metal of my chopper were echoing all around me. I knew it was going to be a difficult take off, but staying here would be suicide. The SEALs started to fire back as I lifted up off the ground. I knew I just needed to get us high enough to where the tangos' bullets wouldn't be able to reach.

As we continued to climb, I started to head off toward the mountains directly in front of us. I had to get around the mountains and then we would be in a safer airfield and I could get these guys back to the base.

"RPG! Take 'em down!" one of the guys, Parker, I believe, called out and I was instantly swearing.

Of course they had RPGs, because that

was the one piece that we were missing to turn this mission into a complete fucking disaster. RPGs could travel a lot fucking farther than a bullet, and they also had the power to bring this chopper down and kill us all.

I couldn't focus on that though, I needed to trust that the guys would be able to shoot the tangos down before they could get one of those RPGs released. All of my hope went right out the window though, when I rounded the mountain and was just able to make out the tango standing on the side of it with an RPG launcher aimed right at us.

I didn't have the time to maneuver us out of the direct path of the RPG as the second we rounded that corner, the tango had released the RPG and it was heading directly toward us.

"Hold on, we're going down!" I shouted before the RPG even hit us. I couldn't avoid it, but I could give the guys behind me the best chance they had to brace themselves for the impact of the RPG and the spinout I was going to have to fight against if I wanted to land this bird down without getting us all killed.

I gripped my stick with everything that I had as the RPG hit the tail of my bird. The second the tail was blown off, we were spinning out of control and heading for the ground at a rapid descent. Alarms were going off from the dash, as if I didn't fucking know we were going down.

The guys were all banging around in the back and I was hoping that they had managed to strap in to prevent them from being sucked out of the two sides. I couldn't think about that right now though,

I had to focus all of my energy to keep us from impacting the ground at the wrong angle that would cause the engine to blow up.

As the ground rapidly approached, it was getting harder for me to hold onto the stick as the whole chopper shook. When the left side of my bird hit the ground we bounced before skidding across the rough desert ground. When we finally came to a stop I was frozen in place. My head was pounding and it felt like my heart was going to break through my chest. There was smoke coming off of the engine and I knew we had to get moving before the diesel in the engine blew up.

Forcing my body to move, I unclicked the seatbelt as I looked over to see that my co-pilot was dead. His empty eyes were looking out the front windshield with his neck at an unnatural position. The impact to the ground had killed him.

Slowly and carefully, I moved out of my seat to see some of the guys had survived. They were all injured, and three were missing, which meant they had gotten sucked out during the descent.

"We gotta move," I said as I went over to the first guy that I could to help him get up and out. It was only a matter of time before those tangos started to make their way toward us to finish what they started.

Out of the ten of them that I had picked up, only four were alive. I knew they wouldn't want to leave their fallen brothers, but we didn't have a choice, we had to move.

We were all injured, but we didn't let that slow us down. The second we got out of the chopper, we were moving toward a series of hills. We needed to get to high ground so we could pick off the tangos while we waited for help to arrive.

I looked over to my right to make sure the guys were all still moving, only to see the SEAL closest to me getting shot in the head and dropping to the ground.

"Xavier!"

I looked around, trying to see who was calling my name, who needed help, but all I could see were the bodies of the SEALs bleeding out.

"Xavier! Wake up!"

There was that voice again, but wake up?

I wasn't asleep, who the fuck could sleep through this?

I had to get to higher ground; it was my only chance at survival. I took off at a sprint, but the ground started to shake and each step I took threatened to bring me down to my knees. A sharp pain through my lower left side of my stomach caused me to drop to the ground. I could feel the wetness of my own blood soaking through my shirt. Black spots started to dance before my eyes and before I even knew it, the darkness overtook me.

"Xavier!"

My eyes snapped open at the sound of my name. There was someone touching me, a tango, he was on top of me. Instantly, I was wrapping my hands around his neck and flipping us so I was straddling his hips with him underneath me. He might have been the tango who shot me and I was not going to allow him to get another chance in.

He squirmed underneath me, his hands going to my arms, hitting my forearms trying to break my hold on his neck. When that didn't work, he started to move his left hand around on the ground, but he wasn't going to find anything in the desert that he could use as a weapon.

The side of my head exploded as I heard glass shatter and it was enough for me to loosen my grip for a moment. The blow to my head was quickly followed by a swift kick to my gut, pushing me back off of the tango and into a boulder, a smooth and cold boulder.

Wait, what was a boulder doing in the desert?

It was cold underneath my arm, it shouldn't be cold.

"Xavier? Baby?" A rough voice broke through my confusion, a voice I knew, but it didn't sound right.

Gage.

What the fuck was Gage doing here in the desert?

"Baby, are you with me? You're in California. We're in your apartment."

No, that didn't make any sense. I was just in the desert. My bird had just been shot down. I had been shot. They were coming for me. I couldn't be in California.

I blinked a few times to try and clear the fog that had invaded my mind. My head was killing me and my stomach was not too happy. My whole body hurt and I felt clammy and gross. I opened my eyes and I was no longer surrounded by desert, but in my own bathroom.

My hand wandered over to my left side where the bullet had torn through it, but there was no blood, no pain. I looked over to where Gage was and instantly my heart dropped to my stomach. He had bruising already coming through on his neck.

Bruising I had put there.

Fuck.

It wasn't a tango that I was attacking, it was Gage.

"Gage, I'm so sorry," I immediately said as the tears started to build up in my eyes.

I could have killed him.

He slid over to me without any hesitation and reached out and pulled me against his chest as he spoke. "It's okay, you didn't know it was me. It's okay. I'm okay."

This wasn't okay. I had put my hands around his neck; I had tried to kill him. None of this was okay and he shouldn't be trying to comfort me right now. He should be horrified and running out of here and never looking back.

"I'm sorry," I said again as I fought with the tears. I was normally able to control my emotions better, but I couldn't right now. Maybe that was because of the withdrawals, but either way, I couldn't seem to lock my emotions back up.

"You don't have anything to be sorry for. I'm okay. You didn't know it was me." He placed a kiss on the top of my head as he ran his hand up and down my back.

The fact that he was trying to comfort me after my hands were just wrapped around his throat only cut me deeper, because he genuinely was a good man and I had hurt him. I had almost killed him. I knew I had demons. I knew getting sober and working through them wasn't going to be easy, but I never suspected that I could attack someone who was trying to help me. That I could dream so deeply that I thought I was back there. It all felt real. I remembered everything with perfect clarity, as if I went back in time and was reliving it again.

How the fuck was that even possible?

"I don't know what happened. I thought you were a tango. I don't know what happened." I shakily pulled back from Gage's embrace. I was feeling waves of heat overtaking me and I was worried that my stomach was going to flip on me again and the last thing I wanted to do was throw up on him.

"You had a flashback. It's common with PTSD. The withdrawals most likely triggered it. It's why when you go through the process of getting sober it's important to speak with a therapist afterward to help reduce and eliminate triggers," he calmly explained, but his voice was still rough.

"It's never happened before."

Why would I have a flashback after all of this time?

I knew some vets had flashbacks or even locked in memories, but that had never happened to me. It was part of the reason why I never believed the Shrink I had to go and see after I got out when he said that I had PTSD. I had no signs, at least none that I would consider to be connected to PTSD. I knew I was fooling myself, but at the time it was just easier to believe that I was fine, that the shrink didn't know what they were talking about. Now I was getting a dose of reality slapped right across my face.

"That's not uncommon. Your drinking most likely has been treating your PTSD symptoms and now that you are not drinking they are starting to appear. I know it doesn't feel like it, but it's actually a good thing."

"How the fuck is almost killing you a good thing?" I couldn't help but snap at him. For fuck's sake, I had my hands wrapped around his throat, squeezing the life out of him. None of this was okay. None of this was a good sign.

"It means you are finally on the road to healing. I'm not saying it won't be hard and it will get worse before it gets better, but now there is a real chance that it will get better. You just need to remember that you are doing this for your son. So you can help him overcome his own demons. If you can get through to the other side of this, then everything that happens will be worth it."

I wished I had even a fraction of the strength and belief that he had, but right now I couldn't get the image out of my head over what happened not even five feet from where we sat. I knew going through withdrawals would be dangerous for me, but I didn't think I would become dangerous to other people.

What if I was in class or worse, in the air, when a flashback hit?

How could I trust myself not to cause harm to someone else?

It was my job as a pilot to ensure the safety of everyone on board my bird and right now, I was the biggest threat to their safety.

How the hell was I going to be able to trust myself with their lives while in the air again?

"Don't, don't do that. I can see it all

over your face that you are doubting yourself. That you are already thinking worst-case scenarios and you need to stop. Right now you are sick, in pain and exhausted, everything is going to appear so much worse than it truly is to you right now. The best thing you can do is focus on the next two weeks and getting your body physically healthy again and recovered from the withdrawals. Then you can start to worry about everything else that comes after it. Starting with a shower. It will help with your withdrawals and it might make you feel a bit more human." He offered me a warm smile and I still couldn't believe he wasn't running out of here. A shower did sound good though, and maybe it would help to make me feel a bit better.

I gave a slight nod and Gage helped me

to get my sweat-soaked shirt off. The second the air hit my damp skin, I felt goosebumps overtaking every inch of my bare body. I still couldn't understand how I could be hot and cold all at the same time.

"You know, this is vastly different to what I thought the first time I would be able to actually see you naked would look like," Gage teased as stood up.

"You have seen me naked," I countered as I slowly pushed myself to my feet.

"No, I've felt you naked. I've never actually seen you in the light. We were naked in the cave and then under a damn bar parking lot light, I barely could see anything. I had hoped the next time would be sexy ripping each other's clothes off type of naked and less Nurse Ratched."

"You don't find nurses sexy?" Despite

how horrible I was feeling, the fact that he had been thinking about being with me again had my blood pooling down to my cock.

"No, and I don't understand what makes them so sexy? I mean, if you need a nurse it's because you're in the hospital either sick or seriously hurt. The last thing I'm thinking about while laid up in a hospital bed is having sex," he commented as his hands went over to my belt and started to open it for me, which I was thankful for because I couldn't get my hands to stop shaking.

"I don't know. You are looking pretty sexy right now." I couldn't help but flirt.

"And you have looked much better. Once you are feeling more human, then we can revisit this discussion on what is sexy," he easily countered, flashing me a warm smile and I couldn't help the light chuckle that slipped from my lips.

He was right about that. I was far from sexy right now, but I was looking forward to getting to do something more x-rated with him in the future. If nothing else, that was one hell of a motivation to reach the end of these two weeks so I would be healthy again physically and we could hopefully move forward and have sex this time around. Our last time opened his eyes, at least I hoped it had, that being a bottom with me could bring him to a whole new level of pleasure. Now, I just needed to be able to handle giving him that experience.

One thing was for certain, these next two weeks were going to be some of the longest weeks of my life.

CHAPTER TWENTY-ONE

Gage

"WE'RE ALMOST AT the drop zone, everyone get ready."

Hearing Xavier's strong, gruff voice bark out orders was like music to my ears. It had been a long two weeks with balancing between my course work and Xavier's withdrawals. He never let me miss a single day in school, but every night I would go over to his place, usually with soup, and make sure he was doing okay.

I knew withdrawals from any substance were brutal on your body and I wanted to make sure that he was recovering properly. I was very relieved after four days when he started to make a turn for the better. He was able to eat more than soup and he wasn't throwing up as much. After a full week, he had a bit more energy and he was coming back to life. All were good signs.

Today he was back to work and I was very happy to have him back, because not only did I get to look at his sexy ass all day, but we were back up in his chopper and getting to make up for the lost time with our practical training.

If Jackson suspected he had more

than the flu for the past two weeks, he didn't give any indication. I had a feeling he knew, but he seemed to care for Xavier and he wasn't about to report him to the Upper Brass.

I strapped myself into the repel harness as we neared our drop zone location. Today, we were practicing going up and down the repel line, plus picking up a dummy and using the basket to simulate a real life rescue. All of the guys were excited for it and couldn't wait to get started.

We could only go up in groups of five and this time I got to be in the first group. I wasn't certain how Xavier would feel about flying so soon after his withdrawals, but he seemed ready for it. We hadn't really talked about his flashback and I knew he was still feeling guilty about trying to kill me. I had meant what I said, it wasn't his fault. He wasn't aware of his actions. He thought I was someone who was trying to kill him and his body did what it was trained to do. I wasn't about to hold that against him, even though I knew others would have.

Getting to class the next day was an interesting time. It wasn't like I had a turtleneck or makeup that I could use to hide the fact that there was bruising all around my neck. There were obviously questions and I had lied and said I stepped in to break up a fight at a bar and got hurt for my troubles. It was believable enough, or the guys were at least nice enough to allow me the privilege of the lie. Either way, I was relieved that it hadn't turned into a big deal.

"All right, we're at the drop zone. I will

hover here. You are going to go one at a time all the way down and wait until everyone else has gone. Then you will come back up one at a time. Mick is going to control the rigging for you. Remember to go at a steady pace," Xavier advised.

Mick was one of the firefighters from the station house up here. He had come by to help us with the repel gear so all of us could get to go down without one of us having to always work the rigging gear.

I hooked myself into the line and turned around before stepping down onto the landing skid. Grabbing my line with both hands, I bent down before pushing off from the landing skid and started to lower myself down to the ground. I had about a hundred feet before I would reach the ground and I knew from my repelling class that I couldn't go too fast on the way down or I risked landing wrong and breaking a bone in my foot or leg. I also didn't want to go too slow, because if this was a real forest fire, I couldn't be dangling above the fire in the air.

I kept an eye on my pace and once I was close enough to the ground, I put my feet down and landed perfectly. I unhooked myself and then stepped back to allow the next cadet to come down.

This was the type of stuff that I liked to do. The chance to utilize my skills and to be able to use the same skills for various situations to help more people. This was making up for all of the long hours sitting in a classroom feeling like a moron. And to make this day even better, Xavier was taking me out for dinner as a thank you for helping him through his withdrawals for the past two weeks.

He didn't need to thank me. I had enjoyed spending the time with him, even if it was while he was sick. Not only had I gotten to get to know him a bit more on a personal level, it had also helped to take my mind off of Asher and Greyson being out in the world on their own. And if all went well tonight, we would be going back to his place after dinner for quite possibly the best sex of my life.

CHAPTER TWENTY-TWO

Gage

I MADE MY way down to the parking lot of the dorms. It was nearing seven at night and Xavier was coming by to pick me up.

We had worked all day long doing practical drills and we both wanted to take a shower and get changed before heading to dinner. I was really hoping it would be a quick dinner followed by a very sexy dessert. I also had no idea where he was taking me, but this was his town and I trusted that he wasn't taking me to some vegan restaurant.

As excited as I was to be going on this date, I was also nervous. It had been a long time since I had gone on a date. Actually, if I was being honest, I'd never really gone on a date, not an official one. There had been times I'd had sex with a guy and then we were both hungry so we went out for a burger, but I wouldn't count that as a date. I'd never really had a boyfriend. There was no time growing up with working and taking care of the twins. Then when things got easier with the twins, I discovered sex and dating didn't seem important. Now, I was twenty-five and going on my first real date, which was pretty sad.

I spotted Xavier's truck pulling up and ambled over to it, quickly jumping into the passenger seat. The second the door was closed, he reached over and placed his hand on the right side of my face and pulled me in for a kiss. This was what I had been dying for. We hadn't done anything since that night in his truck and I was in desperate need to feel him against me again. To be able to taste him.

I felt his tongue against my lips, seeking entrance, and I simply granted it to him. Our tongues fought for control, for dominance, and this time around I wasn't going to give it up to him that easily. He could be in control later.

I moaned as he deepened the kiss and I briefly thought to say fuck it to dinner and just go back to his place for some very delicious dessert. All too soon for my liking, Xavier pulled back and broke the kiss.

"Hi," he said, flashing me a smirk. He was clearly proud of himself for getting me all hot and heavy.

"I'm suddenly starving for something much more fun than food."

He let out a deep chuckle before he spoke. "Oh, trust me, what I have planned for you is going to require you to fuel up first."

"Or we could go back to your place, have some fun, then fuel up before having more fun," I counter offered.

"Now that is very tempting, but the second I get you into my bed, I'm not letting you out until morning," he said with a wink, before he moved away from me and shifted his truck into drive.

I was really hoping that was a promise. Hell, I would be happy to be late tomorrow if it meant some morning delight first. I put my belt on and sat back as Xavier drove us to a restaurant. With this being my first real date there was one thing I needed to know first.

"Are you out?"

"What?" he asked, glancing over at me with his brows slightly furrowed.

"I'm out as gay. I'm not hiding who I am. I just wanted to know if you were also out."

I was terrified of what answer he was going to give. If he wasn't out, then that meant we would have to hide this growing relationship. That shouldn't bother me considering in two weeks I was going to be back home and he would be here. We wouldn't really get to see each other again. I didn't even know if Xavier wanted something more than just a month long fling. At the same time, if he said he was out, I was worried that would make me like him even more. Out and proud firefighters were not very common, although more recently they were finding the courage to come out, be true to themselves, and it spoke volumes about the type of men they were.

"I guess I'm out. I don't know. I've never stated that I was gay, but I've never said I wasn't. Jackson knows and most of the guys that I work with know. I'm not screaming my status from a rooftop, but I'm not hiding either. It certainly wasn't instant. I had kept my orientation a secret all through high school and then in the Air Force. When I got to the fire department, I still kept quiet about it at first, but then Jackson caught me with a guy in an alley, then another guy that I worked with did. There were never any problems over it, so I stopped worrying about someone catching me."

I couldn't stop the smile that spread across my face. He was like a lot of the other guys that I knew that were gay in the department. They were more focused on being themselves than trying to pin a cape to their shoulders and be a spokesperson for homosexuality in first responders. It was good though, it meant we wouldn't have to pretend to be friends if someone spotted us at dinner. It also meant another small piece of my heart was lost to him.

"That's good to hear. I'm out too."

He gave me a rich smile in return. "I figured. When did you come out?"

"I knew when I was a young teenager that I was gay and I told my mom pretty quickly. The twins grew up knowing I liked guys so I didn't have to come out to them. With the department, technically the first day in the academy when I gave my PT instructor head after a very rigorous workout."

"What?" he asked, shocked, but there was also a mixture of jealousy that I detected in his voice.

"You know that I've been with other instructors and firefighters. He was very much in the closet and it was only a one-time thing. I felt very dirty when I discovered he had a wife and three children at home. I've never hidden that I was gay and there have been problems that came up over the years with bigoted assholes, nothing ever serious though." I had lucked out that I ended up in a firehouse with other gay firefighters and my Captain was also gay. It made being true to myself a lot easier.

"I'm glad that you haven't had any problems with anyone, at least not any major problems. Though, I don't like the thought of you with any other instructors, or another man for that matter."

The slight jealous tone did not go unnoticed. Now would have been the perfect time to speak up and ask him about when I went back home in two weeks, but my fear of his answer had won out over my curiosity. I knew it was a conversation we were going to have to have, but it didn't need to be tonight.

When we arrived at the restaurant, a gourmet burger joint, Xavier parked his truck and we headed inside. I loved a good burger so I was really looking forward to getting our food. We grabbed a spot out on the back patio and I was pleased that it wasn't all that busy right now. I wanted to be able to talk freely with Xavier without having to worry about someone overhearing us.

The second we sat down, the hostess took our drink order, both of us getting water.

"You know you could have ordered a drink. I have to get used to people drinking around me," Xavier said, flashing me a warm smile.

"I know, and yes, you do need to get used to being around alcohol and not have any. But I just watched you spend the past two weeks feeling like shit and getting healthy again. I'm not about to test the waters. I don't need to drink to have a good time, not to worry. Plus, I have a feeling I am going to need the hydration for later," I added with a flirty smirk and I was rewarded with a rich smile for my effort.

"Before things go much further between us, there is something I wanted to talk to you about," he started with a serious tone, and I couldn't help but worry about what he wanted to talk to me about before we even got to have sex.

"It's about the flashback."

"I already told you that it was okay. That it wasn't your fault," I instantly cut him off. I didn't want him worrying that I would hold it against him or that I would be scared of him. I didn't really have much experience with PTSD, but I knew the signs and a little about it from work. With Greyson going into the military, it was something I would be doing more research on so I could be better prepared should Greyson develop PTSD himself.

"I know. I did some research and the best way to prevent a flashback from happening again is to talk about it. I have an appointment with a shrink tomorrow, but I hoped to talk to you about it, if you were interested in hearing it," he explained, and I could hear the self-consciousness slipping into his body now. It was obvious he expected me to tell him I didn't want to hear it, but that couldn't have been further from the truth. I wanted to know everything about him and if he was willing to share with me, then I was more than happy to listen to him all night.

"I will always be interested and willing to hear about anything from your past, present, or future." I *really* wanted to know about his plans for the future.

"Being in the Air Force, it was different compared to the on the ground troops. We had our own dangers, but you could also fool yourself into thinking you were in a safer position than on the ground troops. There had been a lot of operations where someone was bleeding out in the back of my bird. A lot of close calls with RPGs and heat-seeking missiles. There had been times where I couldn't go in and pick up the troops, when the area was too hot, and I couldn't get clearance to go in."

"It had to have been hard for you though, to know that people needed help and you couldn't help them." I couldn't even imagine what it must have felt like to be told that you couldn't go in and rescue people. I was thankful that so far in my career, I hadn't had a fire where I had been ordered to stay out of the building. It happened though, sometimes the fire was just burning too hot and moving too fast that sending anyone in to rescue the people trapped inside would only bring more casualties. I knew some of the older guys that I worked with had been in that position and it had destroyed some of them. A few were able to continue working, but the majority couldn't handle the guilt that ate away at them. I suspected that Xavier was living with survivor's guilt and that was making his PTSD worse. It was something that his therapist would have to help him work through.

"It was. We had always been taught that you didn't leave a brother behind and I was right there and couldn't help them.

But if I went against my orders, then I was putting more people at risk. There was one operation that stands out the most to me and that was what the flashback was," he admitted with some pain starting to edge into his voice.

I reached over and took his hand in mine as I spoke, "What happened, baby?"

He sucked in a shaky breath before he spoke. "I was sent to pick up a SEAL team that was pinned down with enemy combatants surrounding them. I wasn't even able to land to load them on, they had to repel up, but it wasn't a typical repel line like you've been on. It's one line with multiple hooks along it so a whole team can hook on and everyone gets brought up while you fly away."

"That sounds dangerous for everyone involved." I couldn't imagine being on a line, just dangling in the air with gunshots going off all around me. I didn't even want to think about Greyson doing any of it.

"It is, but sometimes it's the only option we have. We can't always land a chopper where the troops are, especially the Black Ops guys." He let out a sigh before continuing. "That day everything was going wrong. What pissed me off though, was I got them all on board. We were feet away from being in the clear when the RPG hit. I did my best to land us without the chopper going up in flames, which I did, but not all of the guys had the chance to get strapped in before we got hit. I lost a couple on the way down. They flew right out while we were spinning. By the time we landed, most of the guys were dead. I was able to get out with who was left. We were in a valley in between a couple mountains. We needed to get to higher ground if we were going to stand a chance. We never made it through. The insurgents were ready for us. I got shot; you've seen the scar. It gets a bit fuzzy, but an insurgent reached me and it all went black."

He paused again and I could tell that what he was going to say next was still extremely painful for him and I suspected it was the cause of his PTSD. At least what pushed it into overdrive. I didn't doubt for a second that he didn't have some level of PTSD before the event. He cleared his throat and finished his story.

"When I woke up, I was in this cave with a couple of the other guys. They beat me up pretty good and waterboarded me. They didn't do anything too extreme, they knew by the patch on my uniform that I was just a pilot. I was the guy sent in to pick up the SEALs. I wouldn't have been briefed on their mission. But because of that, I had to watch as the few remaining SEALs that I was tasked to rescue, to get them safe, were tortured and killed. It took about three weeks before we were rescued and by then, it was just me. The Upper Brass had already filed the paperwork for me to be discharged before I even hit the hospital."

My heart hurt for him. I knew war was horrific. Everyone had heard the horror stories; it was why I was terrified of Greyson going over there, even in a medic position. No one was safe and I would be left home hoping that my phone didn't ring or I opened my door and saw some stranger in a suit standing on the other side. I had no idea how I was going to get through any of it.

"I'm so sorry. I know that doesn't really help or offer much comfort, but I am sorry you had to experience it. I don't know how you came back from something like that and yet you have. I know it might not feel like it to you, but look at where you are, baby. You have a job. You're still able to do the thing that you love, flying. You can still help people. I have to imagine that most people who have gone through what you did, have seen the things you have, they wouldn't be able to hold a job, an apartment, getting sober. I know it might not seem like a lot to you, but it's huge, baby."

I didn't want him thinking that the strides he'd made to get better were nothing. It was everything to him and I knew it would be everything to Dexter as well. It takes a strong person to get sober and start therapy all with the hope of getting healthy. He should be proud of himself.

"I don't have a choice, I have to be there for my son. I think if I didn't have Dex, then I probably would have given up long ago," he said, before he paused and I could tell he was getting his thoughts and emotions back in control. "How are your brothers?"

"They are doing really good, surprisingly. I wasn't too certain how long either of them would last, but Asher is loving the ranch, though I think he has the hots for his boss. As for Greyson, he's hanging in. He's acing his in-class work and he is passing the physical aspects. I guess a few of the guys are helping him with it. They both are in good spirits," I said with a small shrug. I still hadn't gotten over the idea of them not being home when I got back. I also was still trying to process Greyson being in the Army. At least they were happy though, and not regretting their decisions.

"Good for them. It's not easy to start a new life and they have both embraced it. Not many kids at eighteen do that anymore."

"A huge part of me wishes they were still tucked away safe at the house. I know I can't keep them forever, but it's hard to let them go."

"I wish I could tell you it gets easier, but it doesn't. But it will become normal."

I wasn't certain that was something I wanted, but I knew I would have to adapt regardless. They were growing up and there was nothing I could do about that. All I could do was be there for them when they needed help.

Pushing all of that aside, I focused on our date and what was hopefully going to come tonight.

CHAPTER TWENTY-THREE

Xavier

I OPENED MY front door and allowed Gage to walk in first.

The rest of dinner had gone great and I would have been happy to take Gage back to the dorms if he wasn't certain he wanted to do anything tonight. He had assured me though, that he did want to come back to my place, and I was so happy, I could have done a dance.

"Do you want a drink?" I asked.

He strolled over to me, placed his hand on my chest, and pushed me back against the door as he spoke. "You don't have to treat me like a delicate flower. The only drink I need is from your cock. Though, I would prefer for it to be in my ass. So why don't you shut up, and fuck me already?" He flashed me a sexy smirk.

That was all I needed to hear.

I flipped us around and slammed him against the door. I spoke as I slid my hand up his chest and lightly placed it over his neck. "Oh, I'm going to fuck you. I'm going to show you exactly how much of a needy submissive bottom you truly are."

"Only for you." He let out a soft, breathy moan.

GAGE

"You're fucking right only for me."

I slammed my lips against his in a dominant and rough kiss. He quickly melted against me and effortlessly submitted to my authority and power. This was something we had both been waiting for and I didn't want to drag it out any longer.

We both quickly worked on divesting the other of their clothes. I guided Gage back toward my bed and we both collapsed down onto it. I broke the kiss and started to kiss and nibble my way down Gage's chest, stomach, and when I reached his hard cock, I ran my tongue along it from base to tip, gathering the pearl of precum from the slit. Gage let out a deep moan, writhing under my ministrations.

I took Gage's cock into my mouth all

the way down to his base as I reached over and grabbed the lube and quickly coated three fingers. I slowly pushed my index finger into Gage's hole and he relaxed his muscles for me.

Gage's hands moved to the bed sheets and clenched them tightly as I added a second finger and really started to work his ass open for my cock. I knew he wasn't going to last much longer. He was too worked up and he wasn't the only one. My cock was rock hard and pulsing with the need to feel him wrapped around me.

"I'm gonna," Gage started, but when I hit his sweet spot, he couldn't manage to get the rest of the words out when he gave a deep moan, more slick precum trickling from the head of his shaft.

I hummed my appreciation over Gage's

hardness, sending vibrations down his cock as I took him down to his base and hit his sweet spot once again. I felt his whole body tense up as his cock pulsed in my mouth and his sweet cum flooded over my tastebuds. I swallowed everything that he had for me and I didn't stop even after he finished pulsing.

I slipped a third finger into his channel and truly started to stretch him out. By the time he was ready for me, he was a writhing and moaning mess on my bed, but that was exactly how I wanted him. The moans that were coming from Gage were driving me insane and I wasn't going to be able to last much longer.

I reluctantly pulled my mouth off his dick and removed my fingers from his sweet ass. He gave a whine at the loss of contact, but I knew shortly he was going to be screaming for more.

I reached over and grabbed a condom, quickly slipping it down over my dick. I then grasped the latex-covered hardness with my lube-covered hand and slicked it up just to make sure that this didn't hurt at all for him. I lined my tip up with his ass as I spoke. "You ready?"

"Fuck, yes," he said, need dripping from his voice. He might not have bottomed before, but he was confident in what he wanted and that helped to ease the slight nerves I was having. I didn't want Gage to regret this.

I gently began to push inside him, pushing through the first tight ring of muscle and breathing heavily with my effort to remain in control. I wanted to pound the hell out of him, but I knew I had to go slow at first. I had to make sure

Gage adjusted to my size as my cock finished stretching him out.

Gage panted as each glorious inch of my cock was pushed inside of him and I had to fight with everything in me to stay at my slow pace. When I finally bottomed out, we were both breathing heavily and I could see that Gage was doing his best to adjust to this new sensation of having my cock in his ass.

"You okay, baby?" I asked as I bent forward and started to kiss along his neck.

"Fuck, you feel good, but also weird," he said with a slight huff of a laugh.

"That weird feeling will pass once you're used to it. The question is, do you want it slow and sweet or hard and fast?"

"I don't want you to hold back. I want to feel all of you and I want to feel your desperate need and passion."

I could see the desire burning in his eyes and I knew he meant every single word he said. And that was all I needed to hear before I pulled out almost all of the way and quickly slammed right back inside. Gage let out a soft scream as my cock nailed right into his sweet spot. I didn't go all out on speed, not yet, he did need to get used to the feel of it first, but that didn't mean I couldn't go hard.

"Oh fuck." Gage whimpered, thrusting his hips even as his back arched up in pleasure. He wrapped his legs around my hips and held on tight. I could feel his legs trembling from the pleasure and I knew he would already be getting close to coming again. I loved how responsive he was to me. It had been a very long time since I had been with anyone who was this desperate with desire and need. As I felt him loosen up, I knew he was ready for me to stop holding back.

I quickly pulled out of him and Gage whined at the loss of pleasure. Before he even had a chance to say anything, I flipped him over and he instantly got down on his hands and knees and put his ass out on display for me. The second his knees touched the mattress, I lined my cock up and slammed right back inside of his perfect ass. Gage gave a long moan as the pleasure overtook his body and his arms gave out and he collapsed onto the bed.

"You like that, baby?" I asked with a smirk.

"Fuck, don't stop. You feel so good," Gage mewled.

I placed my hands on his hips and

started to pound into him with everything that I had, nailing his prostate with each thrust. Gage couldn't stop moaning and whimpering, his hands fisting the sheets, and I knew it wouldn't take long before he was coming without me even touching his cock.

I kept my pace hard and fast, making sure my cock was fully buried deep inside of him with each thrust. I could feel his walls tightening around my cock as I continued to pound into him. It was only moments later when he gave a loud scream, calling out my name as he came.

"Fuck, Xavier!"

I couldn't help but growl softly as I felt his ass squeezing my cock. I knew with each thrust it would cause him to pulse out more cum, milking him for all he had, and I wished I could have seen it as well.

It only took a few more thrusts before I snapped my hips forward and buried myself completely inside of him as I erupted inside the condom.

"Gage," I moaned through clenched teeth as my body was rocked with scorching pleasure. Black dots danced before my eyes and for a second I thought I was going to pass out from the sheer pleasure alone.

I placed my hand on the wall to help hold myself up as we both were breathing very heavily. I managed to look down at Gage and he was struggling to keep his eyes open. His legs had given out on him from the intense pleasure he had just experienced and had flopped to the sides.

I had just enough strength to slowly pull out of him and toss the condom into the garbage can by my bed before I pulled

Gage over to me and we were both out before my brain could form a single word.

CHAPTER TWENTY-FOUR

Xavier

I HAD BEEN in a lot of uncomfortable situations in my life, but sitting there in a therapist's office might actually be the most uncomfortable place I had ever been. I needed to do it, but I didn't know how I would get through it. The only reason I still sat on the couch was because Dexter was counting on me and there was nothing I wouldn't do for him.

"I'm sure you would rather be in a hundred different places right now," Dr. Heath began.

"You aren't wrong."

"And yet, you are here. Care to tell me why that is?"

"My son, Dexter, means the world to me. He'll be eighteen soon and I don't have much of a relationship with him. It's a complicated story that I'm sure we will get into. Recently though, I tried to reach out to him, to make amends for missing out on so much of his life," I started to explain.

"And how did that go?"

"Not how I expected it would. I thought he would be angry and want nothing to do with me. I expected the hurt, but I wasn't expecting the type of hurt that he was in.

He looked in pain and lost. He said he couldn't have me in his life until I got better. That something horrible happened to him and he couldn't handle my shit along with his own. I asked him what happened, but he wouldn't tell me. He doesn't think I'll be able to handle it. My own son is hurting and I couldn't help him because I'm too screwed up. I have to get better so I can help him."

I knew it probably wasn't the healthiest reason, but it was honest and if this doc didn't like it, well that was too bad for him.

"Sometimes we don't start getting better until someone we love forces our hand. Typically, a therapist is supposed to tell you that you can only get healthy when you choose to. That you can't do it for anyone else. However, sometimes it takes fighting for someone you love to make you want to get healthy. I think fighting for your son is a great place to start," he said, flashing me a warm smile.

That was unexpected, but I was glad that he understood where I was coming from and wasn't trying to give me a lecture about getting healthy for *me* and all of that shit.

"By the look on your face, I take it you've been in therapy before and it didn't go well for you," Dr. Heath said, a small smirk gracing his lips.

"Went through it when I got out of the Air Force before starting at the Fire Department. Got diagnosed with PTSD," I answered with a shrug.

"I take it you don't agree with that diagnosis."

I let out a sigh before answering. "I

guess it's not that I don't agree with it, it's that I don't like it. I know guys who have come back missing body parts, their life completely altered and they can never recover from it. I got to keep all of my parts. I get up and go to work every day and still get to fly my bird. What right do I have to complain?"

"I understand that you feel that way; however, PTSD doesn't discriminate. It's not about who had it worse, it's about trauma and how our brains handle it. If I were to send you for a CT-Scan, we would be able to see the PTSD in your brain scan. It's a real injury that can be healed with time and therapy. PTSD can develop from any trauma that someone goes through. You went to war, that comes with a lot of trauma. Can you tell me a bit about your time in the Air Force?"

"I was in for twenty years. Enlisted right at eighteen and left at thirty-eight. I've done hundreds of missions, most of them turned out okay. A few close calls, but nothing that I couldn't handle," I answered with a shrug, but Dr. Heath apparently wasn't buying it.

"Why did you leave?"

That was what I didn't want to talk about, but I knew I would have to. But I didn't know if I wanted to talk about it so soon.

"How does this work? I tell you about the worst things that happened to me and it magically makes me better?" I couldn't help but be skeptical. I couldn't understand how this was going to help me. I was doing this because I had to, but that didn't mean I believed in it.

"It's not magic. It takes a lot of work on

your part. There is no magic pill that will make it all better. You have to want to be better. You have to put the work in and you have to be open and honest with me and yourself. You survived war, multiple times, you have the strength to survive this. As for how it works, we can do this one of two ways. We can start with the small traumas that are easier to talk about and work our way up. Or we can start with the biggest, it'll be hard, but once you work through it, it will give you the biggest relief. It's completely up to you. You have the control and power here. You dictate what we talk about and how fast we move."

I had no idea how I wanted to do this. Talking about some of the smaller shit would be easier, but then it wouldn't tackle the main reason I kept drinking and I needed to deal with that so I could help Dexter. As hard as it would be, I had to jump into the deep end and just hope I could remember how to swim.

"Since I was discharged, I've been drinking. I drink a lot when I'm not working. What I didn't realize was that I would often call Dex while drunk and leave him a voicemail. It's one of the reasons why he hasn't spoken to me and why he won't tell me what happened to him. I've been sober for two weeks now, but I've had a couple of flashbacks, always the same thing," I began to explain. I knew that I could tell him about the drinking and not have to worry about my job. He wasn't allowed to report anything like that, especially if I was sober and not drinking at work. I hadn't put anyone in danger and I never would.

"First, congratulations on getting sober. Even if you feel like two weeks is nothing, I assure you it's not. I have a bunch of information on AA support groups within the city if you want. I highly recommend that you go. You can't stay sober without a support system and sometimes the best support system is the one with people who are like you. With people that can understand what you are going through in terms of the battle you are fighting."

"I'll take the info. I've already been looking into it."

I had no interest in sitting around and talking about my problems to a group of strangers, but I also knew I couldn't foolishly just assume that I would be the exception and stay sober without putting in any effort for it.

Dr. Heath gave a nod before he continued. "Second, it's not uncommon to have flashbacks with PTSD and the only way you can prevent them from happening again is by talking about what you saw. If you are having a flashback about the same event repeatedly, then that is a major event that is strongly connected to your PTSD. Would you be willing to tell me about it?"

"I've only told one person about it. It's why I was honorably discharged. Most of it is classified, but the down and dirty version is I was picking up some SEALs to get them out of a hot zone. My chopper was shot down and not all of them survived the crash. While trying to get into a safer area, I was shot and we were captured. I spent three weeks trapped in a cave being tortured and the SEALs who had survived the crash were with me. By the end of the three weeks, I was the only one alive when the rescue team arrived. The drinking started when I got home after two weeks in a German hospital before I was cleared to be discharged."

"I'm terribly sorry you had to endure that. I think it's safe to say that traumatic experience is at the core of your PTSD. I would really like to speak to you about it, if you are comfortable with that as your starting point."

"No offense, Doc, it's not really about being comfortable. None of this makes me comfortable. I highly doubt that is going to change. I'm here because I have to be, because my kid needs me to be. If my last operation is what is standing in the way of me being healthy, or me helping my kid, then let's go."

Talking about those three weeks wasn't something I ever wanted to do, but I would do it. For Dexter, I would do it. I was just hoping that I could get through this so I could come out of it stronger and be there for Dexter again. He was relying on me and I was not going to fail him again.

CHAPTER TWENTY-FIVE

Gage

"OH FUCK." I moaned as I leaned my head back against the wall.

I'd arrived a bit early to take my final exam this morning. I wanted some time to pace around and try to work off some nervous energy before I would need to sit down and focus on the exam. Only, Xavier appeared to have a different idea to work off my energy.

He'd pulled me into one of the supply closets and took my cock deep down his throat. My hand was threaded through his hair and my eyes were locked on him. I still couldn't believe he could take me all the way in his mouth. His throat felt so fucking good, so tight and hot. It was just like fucking someone's ass. I was going to miss that, but I wouldn't trade the feeling of Xavier's cock in my hole for anything.

He locked eyes with me as he took me deep and moaned his appreciation. The vibrations sent a shockwave of pleasure right up my spine and I couldn't help but thrust my hips forward just slightly. I didn't want him to choke, but I also wasn't willing to give up my complete control either. I watched as he reached down and started to jerk himself off as I fucked his throat.

"You feel so good. So tight and hot. You look so fucking sexy with my cock down your throat. Fuck, you're gonna make me come soon."

I couldn't help but pick up my pace. Xavier kept moaning and the vibrations were driving me up the wall. I loved seeing him like this. I loved knowing I could get him this wound up. That I could make him this needy. I could tell he was getting close as his moaning picked up and I could see his hand moving faster. He wasn't the only one who was close.

"Come for me, baby." I grunted as I fought to hold off. I wanted him to fall off the cliff first. I wanted to watch as he came with my cock down his throat.

It only took a few more seconds before he let out a long and deep moan around my cock as his own exploded with his orgasm. The sight of it pushed me over the edge and I thrust my hips forward once more before I came hard down his throat. I hissed at the sensation of his throat constricting around me as he swallowed everything I had for him. We both continued to pulse as we rode out our high and after a moment Xavier pulled back.

"Well, that's one way to start the day," I said with a slight huff of a laugh.

"I had to make sure you were relaxed for your test," Xavier said as he kissed his way back up my stomach and over to my neck.

"I hope you aren't doing this with all of your students," I teased, but in reality I was now back to being stressed and worried about the final exam.

I still couldn't believe it had already been a month. It felt like time had zoomed past me. I wasn't ready to leave. I wasn't ready to leave Xavier or face all of the unknowns about our relationship.

Was it even a relationship?

Maybe this was more like a summer fling and we would go our separate ways now and never connect with the other again. I really hoped that wasn't the case, but that wasn't something that only I could decide. I hadn't brought it up to him, yet, mostly because I was scared of what his answer would be. He was going through a lot and he had to focus on his mental health so he could be healthier for himself and for his son. I completely understood that needed to be his priority and I wanted him to make it a priority. At the same time though, I really still wanted to be in his life.

"Only you. Though, it wouldn't surprise me if Jackson had someone else in one of the supply closets." I felt his smirk against my neck as he kissed me one last time before he pulled back.

"Jackson gets around, I take it?" I asked, as I started to pull my pants back up.

"It's safe to call him a manwhore. He's a forty-five year old who is trapped in the mindset of a horny twenty year old. He tends to date multiple guys at the same time. One time, he even dated brothers. They weren't twins, so your brothers still take the cake on that, but Jackson has broken a lot of hearts. And he has a gift at sniffing out the gay guy or bi-curious guy in every class."

"I guess it's a good thing it was you

flying that chopper and not Jackson. I couldn't imagine being cuddled up with him in the cave and not you."

I didn't have a problem with Jackson. He was a good guy and he was a very patient teacher. He looked good, especially for his age, but he wasn't Xavier and I couldn't imagine a scenario where I would want to be with him. Where I would want to feel his body against mine. Xavier on the other hand, now he was a man I wanted to do nothing but lay naked with.

"It's hard to believe that was only a month ago. It's hard to believe that in two days you are going to be gone," he said sadly as he moved back and righted his own clothes.

"This course has definitely not gone how I expected it to. It's going to be weird going home to an empty house, going back to work again. I've basically seen you every day for the past month, how am I going to survive not seeing your face every day?" I asked with a teasing smile, but the reality was I hoped he would tell me that I would get to see him again. That he didn't want this to end and we could work something out.

"I know what you mean. Especially this past week. I've gotten used to feeling your body against mine while I sleep. I know we live on opposite ends of the country, but I would like to keep seeing you. If you think you could handle the long distance thing."

I couldn't help the smile that instantly spread across my face. I had never done a long distance relationship, but for Xavier I was all for trying. I didn't know what the future would hold for the two of us, but I was willing to put the work in and see what we could make of this relationship.

"For you, I'm willing to try anything. I think we could make it work."

I had no idea how truly hard it would be, but I was hoping it wouldn't be too hard to adjust to the distance. Once I got back to Baton Rouge, I would be working at the firehouse again and it would hopefully make the days go by faster until I could physically see Xavier again.

"It wouldn't be forever. Maybe six months, a year at most. I have to try and get transferred over to Baton Rouge or close to it. I need to keep going with my therapy right now and start building up a relationship with Dex again."

"Take as long as you need. Your therapy and your relationship with Dex are more important than anything. We can survive off texts and phone sex," I said as I wiggled my eyebrows and it put a smile on his face.

"As much as I would like to explore more about our phone sex options, you have an exam to write in fifteen minutes."

"And now I am back to being nervous, thanks for that," I grumbled as we both headed out of the supply closet.

The exam was not one I was looking forward to. I hated exams to begin with, but anything that had to do with the fire department always made me more nervous. This wasn't some stupid history exam; this was an exam that would dictate what happened with my career. If I failed, I wouldn't be able to take the course again and I would be going back home as a failure. That wasn't something

I could handle happening. I had to pass, but I was truly worried about different parts of the exam. Xavier had been working with me in class and after hours to ensure I understood the material and I would be able to handle any tests. Still, that nervousness seeped into my bones and all I could do at this point was hope for the best.

Xavier grabbed my hand and stopped me from continuing down the hallway. I turned toward him as he looked me dead in the eyes and spoke. "You are ready for this. You know the material. All you have to do is trust yourself. Don't second guess your answers or the process. You're ready, I promise you."

A deep sigh escaped my mouth before I could contain it. Xavier knew about my lack of high school success, but he never judged me for it. He never saw me as stupid, not like I often viewed myself as. He believed in me, even when he had no reason to. I didn't feel ready, but the fact that Xavier told me I was ready did ease my nerves slightly.

"Tonight is our last night together for who knows how long and I plan to make sure it is a very memorable one for you. So whenever you feel stressed or anxious during the exam, just think about me and how good it feels to have my cock pounding into you."

I let out a soft moan before I managed to find my voice. "Now that's all I'm going to be thinking about."

I still couldn't believe how amazing it felt to be a bottom. I never thought I would ever submit to any man, but there was something special about Xavier that made it so easy to do just that. I suspected he was the only man I would ever submit to, but that was just fine by me.

"I'll see you tonight. Good luck."

I could tell he wanted to kiss me, but we couldn't do that out in the open. The last thing either of us needed was someone seeing us and assuming Xavier had shown me favoritism. Any celebrations would have to wait until tonight, but it would at least give me something to look forward to.

Letting out a long breath I turned and started to head back down the hallway to reach the classroom. There was no going back now.

CHAPTER TWENTY-SIX

Gage

MY BRAIN WAS mush. That was the only word I could manage to think of to accurately describe how I felt right now. I had to imagine this was how Asher felt after every exam he had in high school. I was able to finish the exam, but I had no idea how I did on half of it. I didn't need a perfect score, but I hoped I had managed to at least pass it. Honestly though, I wasn't feeling too confident about it.

I collapsed down onto one of the picnic tables out back and pulled my phone out. I sent a quick text off to Xavier letting him know I was finished and I followed it up with a gun emoji and the brain exploding emoji. I knew Xavier would want to talk about it, but right now I wanted to try and reach out to Greyson. I had spoken to Asher a few times over the past month, but I hadn't been able to speak with Greyson. The time shift was killing me. We were literally on opposite ends of the country and by the time I got done in class, Greyson was usually getting ready for bed. It was just after four my time, so I hoped that meant I could catch Greyson before he got ready for bed.

I hit his contact and put the phone to

my ear, listening to the endless number of rings, and just when I thought I was going to be getting his voicemail again, I got the sweet sound of his voice.

"Hey, I was hoping you would call. Asher said you had your final exam today. How did it go?"

Just hearing his voice helped to put my fears at ease. He sounded good. A bit tired, but he didn't sound like he was ready to fake his death just to escape.

"Well, about halfway through I was hoping someone would run in and pull the fire alarm. I have no idea if I passed or not, but now all I can do is wait."

"I'm sure you aced it. You've always been good at these fire courses," Greyson said with complete confidence in me. Too bad I didn't feel that way.

"I'll see. I don't want to talk about me

though; I want to know how you are doing. I've been getting second hand intel from Asher and I love your brother, but he sucks at telephone."

Greyson gave a chuckle at that before he spoke. "He hears what he wants to hear. I've been doing good though. It's not what I expected, but truthfully, I didn't know what to expect. The guys here are really good. I haven't told them much about myself other than I have a twin and older brother. I've been keeping personal details out of it."

"Like that you are gay. Any reason why?"

"I want my skills to speak for themselves. I don't want to be the token gay guy or used as a rung on some political ladder. I want to be like everyone else. Plus, I think it might be easier in the long run to not get too close to anyone. At any given moment they could be killed overseas and it'll hurt less if I don't develop any emotional attachment to them."

"I can understand that would appear to be the easier route, but I don't know how healthy or possible that would be. The one instructor for my course, Xavier, was in the Air Force. He told me that the teams are like a family. Everyone gets close and protects each other. Being part of a team, you're gonna have to open yourself up to the others. You're gonna have to know them to help build trust. I don't think you should shut yourself off to the possibility of a deeper connection to people."

I knew logically what Greyson was saying made complete sense. It would be easier to lose people if you didn't know much about them. If there was no emotional connection to them. However, in practice, that didn't really work out the same way. You couldn't be on a team with a group of people and not know them. Even if you didn't ask them questions, you would still gain information from conversations they had around you. Unless Greyson planned to walk around with noise canceling headphones on, he was screwed.

"I understand what you are saying, but I'm not looking to mourn any losses. As a medic, my job is to keep the patient alive until I can get them to a doctor. It's just like a paramedic getting the patient to the hospital."

"Yeah, but you don't spend weeks or months, hell even years, with that patient as you take them to the hospital. You will be training with your team and doing team bonding exercises and living together when you are overseas. It's a lot more than just patching 'em up." I was worried that Greyson was setting himself up for more heartbreak and failure with how he was planning on handling his connection to his team.

"I'll be fine. You don't have to worry about me," he said in a tight voice and I could tell he was not in the mood for the conversation. I had to let it go and just hope that he would meet his new team once he graduated Boot Camp and it would change his mind.

"I'm always going to worry about you. How has the physical aspect been?"

"It was tough at first, but now I've gotten into a routine with it. My mathematical skills have come in handy with the shooting. I'm at the top of my class in that sense."

"Good... I think," I said with a slight chuckle. I was glad he was doing well, but I didn't know if I wanted a first place trophy in shooting to come home.

"It is good. It means I will be better able to protect myself and my team in the field. I heard Asher is doing well and loves being on the ranch. He's got the hots for his boss. I told him to keep it to his wet dreams and not be stupid."

"Yeah, I practically told him the same thing. Hopefully, he listens to us, but that is a decision only he can make. Are you sure you are okay there? No regrets?"

"I'm sure. I like the work and I know it will be good once I can focus on the medical aspect of my training. I can do that here, so I won't have to relocate until after my training."

"And how long does that take?"

"Anywhere between sixteen and sixty-eight weeks. It all depends on how much specialized training I want to do. I'm not sure yet, but I might go for the full sixty-eight weeks. That way when I eventually leave the Army, I can get a job as an ER doctor or even a trauma surgeon with additional training."

I was not about to tell him not to do sixty-eight weeks. That was just over a year of me not having to worry about him being in the middle east. Another year where he would be safe.

"I think you should get as much training as you can. I mean, you are getting paid to learn, you might as well take advantage of that."

"I will most likely do the full program. It will give me more skills to have when I am out there and a greater chance of saving someone's life. I gotta get going though. I need to shower and then turn in for the night. I have to be up at oh-five hundred."

"Five am, no fucking thank you." I hated mornings and everyone at the firehouse knew that. "I love you and be safe."

"Always. I love you, too and I'll talk to you again in a couple of days. Let me know when you get back home."

"I will. I'm proud of you, Greyson."

"Thanks, big brother. Talk soon."

He ended the call and I let out a long breath. I felt better now that I'd spoken to him, but at the same time I was just as anxious. I knew I had to get used to it. It was Greyson's decision to be in the Army and I had to respect it, even if it made me feel like throwing up.

I scrubbed a hand over my face and forced my body to move. I had to go and pack up my room so I could be ready to leave in two days. I already knew I would be spending the day tomorrow with Xavier so this was truly my only chance to get this done, because there was no way I would be leaving Xavier's to pack up my room. I hoped tomorrow I wouldn't even be wearing clothes. With that happy thought, I headed off for the dorms.

CHAPTER TWENTY-SEVEN

Xavier

I MADE MY way to the park once again where I knew Dexter would be. He had a half day today and I knew he would be at the park playing ball.

I hoped he was alone, because it would be easier to speak with him. If he was in the middle of a game, it would be harder to get him to stop playing and speak with me. Who the hell was I kidding, it was going to be a small miracle if I could get him to talk to me at all.

I knew I wouldn't be able to get him to trust me right away. It was going to take some time and a lot of work to earn his trust back. For him to see that I would be there for him, no matter what happened in the future or what had happened in the past. I desperately wanted to know what demons he was fighting. I hated that he was going through this alone.

I knew he had his mother, but given what little he had told me about her behavior since the divorce, plus what I had experienced with her, I knew she wouldn't be much help at all. Most likely she would send him to church more and pretend like nothing was wrong.

I rounded the corner and I easily heard

the sound of a basketball dribbling. I was also pleased to see that it was only Dexter there and not a group of people. It was still early enough in the afternoon that others hadn't arrived yet. I waited until I was closer before I called out.

"Dex!"

At the sound of his name, he turned around and stopped dribbling. He didn't give me a smile, but he also didn't appear to be annoyed by my presence and I took that as a win.

"What are you doing here?" he asked, but there wasn't an edge to his voice. He actually sounded exhausted.

"I wanted to check in and see how you were. I know I could have called, but I like seeing your face. How are you doing, Dex?"

"Okay, I guess. Shouldn't you be at

work?"

"The new round of cadets are doing their final exam today for the course I teach. I don't have to be there. My partner, Jackson, he watches over them. I mostly teach them up in the air. I got the whole day off. We could play a bit of ball if you want."

"Just because you show up here doesn't mean anything has changed," he simply said.

"I know, and I know I have a lot that I need to make up for. I've been sober for just over two weeks now. I know it's not much, but it's a start. I've also started therapy to deal with my drinking and PTSD. I'm working on getting better so I can be the father that you need. So I can help you with everything you are going through. I want you to feel like you can talk to me. That you can depend on me and know that I'm always going to be there for you."

"And all of that sounds great, but it's only been two weeks," he said with a small shrug. He had every right to be skeptical. I hadn't been there for him and given how much hurt was radiating off of him, he needed the protection of a father and he had been denied that. He was going to need a lot more than two weeks sober before he felt like he could trust me, but I would prove to him that he could.

"I know. And I know it's going to take a lot more than just a couple of weeks, but I am not going to relapse. Those weeks will keep adding up and I will earn your trust back. There's no rush though, Dex. I'll go at your pace." The last thing I wanted was for him to feel like I was pressuring him.

He looked down for a moment, rolling the ball around in his hands before he finally looked up and spoke. "Do you play?"

"I have in the past. Basketball was one of the few activities we could do overseas on base. I'm out of practice though, so you might have to go easy on me," I said, flashing him a warm smile.

"I guess I could." He gave me a small one shoulder shrug, but I also saw a hint of a smile and it warmed my heart to see it. I had a long road to go with him, but I had managed to finally take my first step on that road and it felt amazing.

CHAPTER TWENTY-EIGHT

Xavier

THE SECOND THE door was closed, I pulled Gage in for a heated kiss, one he easily returned. I guided us over toward my bed as we both worked on removing the other's clothing. We only had tonight and tomorrow to spend together and I was not going to waste a single second of it.

The second we were naked I pushed

him down onto my bed. He instantly spread his legs and the sight of him spread out and ready for me, made me moan. I started to place kisses along the inside of his left thigh as I spoke.

"You look so fucking delicious, baby."

I ran my tongue along Gage's thick shaft, causing him to let out a hiss at the contact. We were both so wound up tight and I doubted either of us would last very long at this point. That was okay though. We had plenty of time to take things slow later.

I took Gage's tip in my mouth and sucked on it, moaning at the sweet taste of Gage's precum hitting my tongue, his flavor flooding my mouth. I pulled back and spoke as I reached over to the bedside table and pulled out some lube and a condom.

"Fuck, you taste so sweet. I'm never going to get tired of it."

"I swear I am going to explode soon if you do not get your mouth around my cock," he said with a slight growl.

"So needy, baby," I teased. I lightly licked at his cock, tonguing the slit and lapping up more of his delicious essence.

"Xavier, please, no teasing, not tonight. I just need to feel you," he whined.

I knew he had been stressed out over his final exam and I knew he needed to shut off his mind and to just allow his body to feel what it needed to feel.

"I got you, baby," was all I said, before I took his hard cock all the way into my mouth and I didn't stop until I was completely down to his base. His cock was already rock hard and I knew he was in desperate need to come.

I worked his dick in my mouth as I got three of my fingers slicked up with the lube. I inserted my index finger and I groaned around his cock at how tight his ass was. Gage moaned at the pleasure that I knew was scorching through his body.

I pushed my index finger all the way in before I slowly pulled it out before moving it back in. I felt Gage's hand moving to my hair and he grabbed a chunk of it as he thrust his hips slightly and began to lightly fuck my mouth.

I moaned as I added a second finger and really started to work his hole. I couldn't believe how amazing Gage tasted and how good it felt to feel his cock sliding over my tongue and down my throat.

I focused on stretching him, but I knew he was getting closer to coming. I added my third and final finger and started to search out his sweet spot. I knew it would make him fall off that cliff and I desperately wanted to feel his cock pulse in my throat. I knew I hit it when his back arched off the bed and he let out a sharp cry.

"Oh fuck, Xavier."

I could feel his legs starting to shake with his need to come. I picked up my pace, making sure to take all of his cock down to his base as I rubbed fast circles over his sweet spot. Gage was a writhing, moaning mess on the bed and it was only a moment later when he gave a small scream as he came hard down my throat.

I moaned as his sweet taste flooded into my mouth and trickled down my throat. I greedily swallowed everything that Gage had for me. I continued to work his cock in my mouth as he continued to pulse. I didn't remove my mouth until he finished pulsing, softening slightly, only then did I start to pull off and I gave his tip a hard suck to get every last drop from him. I removed my fingers from his ass as I spoke.

"Fuck, I could drink you all day, baby."

"I'd die a very happy man if you did," he said with a big smile on his face.

I picked up the condom and quickly slipped it on, before I positioned myself at Gage's hole. I placed my hands on the underside of Gage's thighs and held his legs up slightly as I slowly started to push my tip into his stretched hole. I couldn't stop the deep moan that escaped my throat as my tip was engulfed with the heat of Gage's tight ass.

Gage couldn't stop moaning as my

cock slowly slipped inside of him, inch by inch, until I was fully buried inside of him. Once I bottomed out, I had to close my eyes for a moment and allow myself to feel the pleasure coursing through me. His ass felt amazing around my cock and I had to really fight with myself to not pound into him.

"Fuck, baby, you feel so good," I moaned as I fought to control myself.

"So deliciously big. I'm good, move," Gage begged.

"It's not going to be slow," I warned. I couldn't go slow, not right now, not when it felt this good. The next time, I would go slow then.

"Good, I don't want it slow. Fuck me hard, babe. Make me yours."

I didn't need to be told twice. I pulled out almost all of the way and then I slammed right back into Gage's needy ass until I was balls deep once again. The aggression of my thrusts caused him to let out a keening moan and I didn't waste any time before I angled my hips, pulled out and slammed back in, hitting Gage's sweet spot dead on. Gage gave a small scream as the pleasure shot through him once more.

"Oh, I love that sound," I moaned as I picked up my pace. I could listen to Gage's moans and pleasure for the rest of my life and never get tired of it.

Gage wrapped his legs around my hips and it allowed me to pound even deeper and harder into him. His hands made their way to my back and he ran his fingernails down my back, leaving scratches in his wake I was sure.

I continued to pound into Gage hard

and deep. I didn't want this to end, but I could feel myself getting closer. I moved my free hand down to Gage's hard cock that was already dripping with precum once again. The second my hand made contact, Gage let out a whimper as I started to jerk him off in time with my thrusts.

After I hit his sweet spot one more time, Gage screamed my name as he came hard all over my hand, jet after jet of thick white ropes covering my fist and his belly.

The tightening of his walls was enough to push me over the edge and I came hard and deep inside of Gage's ass with a deep moan. We were both breathing heavily as we fought to come down from our high.

I placed my forehead against his as we both fought to catch our breaths. This was only round one and before Gage would need to leave in the next thirty some odd hours, I planned on having as many rounds as humanly possible with him.

EPILOGUE

Six Months Later...
Gage

MY WHOLE BODY radiated with excitement and pure horniness. I stood in the airport with my cock half hard because after six months Xavier was finally coming to visit.

He had been sober for six and a half months and he had been going through intense therapy, but he had a solid grip on his drinking and his PTSD. We'd been talking every day and having a lot of video and phone sex. He planned on moving to Baton Rouge soon, but he wanted to wait until Dexter graduated high school before he made the move. I completely understood and supported his decision.

Things between Dexter and Xavier were still more shaky than not, but they were making progress. We still didn't know what had happened to Dexter, he was keeping that in a very heavily locked box. I knew it was driving Xavier crazy not to know, but he had to wait until Dexter was ready to give that up. I just hoped that it wouldn't be anything too devastating to either of them.

Asher and Greyson were doing great. Greyson had graduated Boot Camp and was focusing on his medical courses. They were both having a great time and I couldn't be more proud of them. It was hard coming home to an empty house. Even something as simple as sleeping was hard. Not falling asleep to the faint sound of Asher's music or hearing them moving around from their room to the bathroom. Even just knowing that I was completely alone made it difficult for me to close my eyes. I had gotten used to it now, but that didn't mean I liked it. Maybe I needed to get a dog or something. That was something else I could figure out another day.

I pushed those thoughts aside as people started to come through the gate. I couldn't stand still as I waited to see Xavier come through the gate. I knew the guys at work all wanted to meet him, but

I took today off for a reason and that was not so we could be around a bunch of guys. I wanted my man in my home, naked, and moaning.

The smile was instantly spreading over my lips as I finally saw Xavier coming toward me. I walked toward him and his arms opened for me. I practically flung myself into them and they were instantly closing around me in a strong hug.

Fuck, he felt amazing.

"Fuck, I missed you," Xavier growled into my neck.

"Me too. Come on, let's get the hell out of here and to my place," I said as I moved back.

"Straight to your place, eh?" he said, flashing me a sexy smirk.

"Would you prefer I take you on a tour of Baton Rouge?" I asked, but I already knew the answer.

"My cock in your tight ass is the only tour I need, baby," he whispered into my ear and it sent a shiver down my spine. Fuck, now I was fully hard in an airport full of people.

We quickly made our way to my car and after tossing his duffle bag into the back seat, we climbed in and headed off for my house. We had been driving for a few minutes when Xavier reached over and began to undo my jeans.

"What are you doing?"

"My mouth is bored," he stated, as if we were talking about the weather. Before I realized what was going on, my pants were open and he was bending forward to run his tongue along my half hard cock, causing me to let out a deep moan.

"You do know I'm trying to drive? And

it's broad daylight, right?" I asked, as he ran his tongue up and down my now extremely hard cock.

"I'm not stopping you," he countered playfully.

Xavier sucked on my tip and moaned his appreciation as the taste of my precum hit his tongue. I did my best to focus on the road as Xavier took my cock into his mouth. I had done a lot of things in my life, but I had never gotten my cock sucked while I was driving. That wasn't something I ever thought I needed to experience and now all I wanted was for Xavier to suck my cock dry the whole way to my place.

Xavier took all of my cock into his mouth, burying his nose in my pubic hairs and sucking in a deep sniff. I moved my hand over to his head and threaded my fingers through his hair. Xavier moaned at the tight grip on his hair as he worked his mouth all up and down my hard cock. Every time he took me down to my base, I gave him a deep moan as my tip hit the back of his throat.

"Fuck, babe." I whimpered as I thrust my hips up slightly.

Xavier sucked hard and the pleasure shot through my whole body. My balls pulled up tight and I felt my orgasm coil in my belly.

"Babe, I'm gonna…"

After a few more seconds, Xavier let out a long moan as I came hard down his throat. Xavier swallowed everything that I had to offer him and when I finished pulsing, he continued to suck my cock. I hissed at the sensitivity, and grabbing a fistful of his hair, I pulled Xavier's mouth off my cock.

"It's sensitive." I said.

"Are we there yet?" Xavier countered.

"No, half way roughly."

"Then I'm not done playing yet," he said with a playful smile as gave my shaft a long lick.

"Oh my god. Fuck," I hissed.

Xavier took my tip into his mouth again and sucked on it, his tongue penetrating my slit and gathering the slick there. I did my best to focus on the road as Xavier worked my cock all over again, getting it just as hard as before. Xavier moaned as he moved up and down my cock before he pulled his mouth off.

"I love how your cock feels against my tongue," he growled before he took my cock back into his mouth.

"Fuck. I'm thinking you have an oral

fixation, babe," I whined as I rested my head against the headrest as I pulled up to a red light. I took a moment to look down and watched for a moment as Xavier worked his mouth all the way down my cock. "Fuck, you are so sexy like that. I could watch you suck cock all day and night long."

I pulled out my cell phone and opened up the camera. I turned the video camera option on and placed my phone on the door handle so I could record Xavier sucking my cock.

"I swear, it'll just be for me," I promised.

Xavier looked right at the camera and gave a deep moan right before he took my cock all the way down to my base. I moaned, ecstatic that Xavier had no problem being recorded. I decided then and there that we would need to make a lot of videos during his visit.

I continued to focus on the road as we got closer to my house. I wanted to come again down Xavier's throat before I would get to feel his massive cock in my ass. I was getting close to coming, but I wanted to do it once I was parked so I could lean back and really feel Xavier's throat around my cock.

Once I finally pulled onto my driveway, I turned the truck off and leaned back in my seat, shifting my hips upward. Xavier could now get a better angle on my cock.

He looked right at the camera as he pulled off my cock and ran his tongue over my tip. He moaned his appreciation as he took my tip into his mouth and sucked on it hard. I moaned as Xavier played it up for the camera. I knew this video would be what I used at night to jerk off to once he went home, along with many others hopefully.

I watched in anticipation as Xavier ran his tongue up and down my shaft slowly before he took me back into his mouth, all the way down to my base. I tightened my grip in his hair once more and started to thrust my hips up, pushing my cock further down his throat.

"Fuck, I'm gonna come down this sweet throat of yours," I hissed as I picked up my pace, marveling at the gagging sounds coming from my lover.

I was so close. I needed to come and then I needed to take Xavier inside and have him fuck the living hell out of me. After another moment, I came once again with a growl as I shot my load down Xavier's throat. Xavier moaned and hummed as the taste of my cum flooded his mouth. He swallowed every last drop that I had to offer him.

Once I stopped pulsing, Xavier moved back off my cock and made sure to suck and lick at my tip, getting every last drop before he gave the camera a wink and then reached over to turn it off. He looked over at me and smirked at seeing how wrecked I was.

"I hope you're not too tired. We're just getting started," Xavier said, flashing me a playful smile.

"I'm never going to be too tired to feel your cock pounding into me," I promised.

I opened the car door and stumbled my way to my front door. I heard the other car door opening and I knew Xavier was right behind me. I headed inside, leaving the door open, and made my way up the stairs to my bedroom with Xavier's footsteps following right behind me. I would give him a tour later.

I removed each piece of clothing as I made my way down the hall to my bedroom, dropping them as I went. By the time I reached my bedroom, I turned around and saw that Xavier was already naked too. He grabbed me by the back of my neck and pulled me in for a deep kiss. I willingly allowed Xavier's tongue to enter my mouth, moaning at the taste of myself all over Xavier's tongue.

I continued to kiss Xavier as we moved back toward my bed and once my knees hit the bed, Xavier carefully lowered us down. I crawled backward on the bed to grant us more room, opening my legs for Xavier to fit between them.

Xavier pulled away from the kiss and

slowly began to kiss and nibble his way down my neck, down my chest, nipping at each hard nipple, and then over my stomach, all the way down to my hard cock once again. I reached over to the bedside table and pulled out the lube and placed it down on the bed.

Xavier took my hard cock into his mouth and he didn't stop until he was all the way to my base. I gave a hiss as the pleasure shot through me and my sensitive cock. I highly doubted he was going to be able to make me come for a third time right now, but I was more than happy to allow him to give it his best shot.

Xavier worked my cock as he slicked up three of his fingers. He ran his left hand up my stomach, my chest, and finally to my throat where he grasped my throat in a light grip as he used his right hand and inserted his index finger into my needy ass. I whimpered, thrusting back against his digits and I couldn't help but roll my eyes back as my body was wracked with pleasure. I loved when Xavier took control over me and he fucking knew it. Xavier pushed his finger in all the way before he slowly pulled it out.

I clenched the bed sheets in my fists as Xavier added a second finger quickly. I couldn't believe how amazing this felt. Xavier worshiped my body like no man had ever done before. The pleasure was so intense I couldn't help but wiggle my hips to try and get more friction from his fingers. After a moment, he added a third finger and started to look for my sweet spot.

"Xavier," I moaned deeply as I felt that

shockwave of pleasure as he hit my sweet spot dead on.

Xavier picked up his pace on my cock, making sure to take all of me down to the base as he rubbed fast circles over my sweet spot. I was a writhing, moaning mess on the bed and it was only a moment later when I let out a small scream as I came hard down Xavier's throat for the third time in the past hour.

Xavier moaned as he greedily swallowed what I had for him, though I had no idea how I still had cum to offer him. He didn't remove his mouth until I stopped pulsing and then he pulled his fingers from my channel as he moved back. I whined at the loss, my hole fluttering on empty air.

Xavier kept his grip on my throat as he moved up and kissed me roughly. I happily allowed him to dominate the kiss and when he slipped his tongue into my mouth, I ran my own tongue over his and moaned at the taste of myself.

I loved that Xavier could be sweet and gentle, but also that he could take charge and be dominant and aggressive. This was exactly what I needed, especially because it was going to be a long time before we would get to be together again once he went back home. Xavier pulled back from the kiss and moved his free hand to snag the bottle of lube as he spoke.

"You sure?" he asked.

"Fuck yes. I want to feel your cock. I want to feel your hot cum shooting into my ass."

We had talked about the possibility of not having a condom the next time we had sex. We were both only seeing each other and we had both gotten tested and the tests came back negative for everything. Not that we had expected to have any surprises with the fact we were both tested regularly as part of the firefighter's health initiative.

I had dreamed about feeling his cock inside of me without any barrier, using the thoughts as jerk off fodder many nights since I'd last seen my lover, and I couldn't wait to finally make that dream into a reality.

Xavier positioned his hips so his cock was notched against my hole. He slowly pushed his tip into my already-lubed hole and I couldn't stop the deep moan that escaped my throat as his tip was engulfed within the tight heat of my ass.

We both had never had sex without a

condom before and now that we were finally getting to experience it, together. I knew after this, condoms were something we were never going to want to go back to.

Xavier pushed in a bit more until he was buried all the way into my ass, his hips tight against my cheeks. Xavier closed his eyes for a moment and I knew he was fighting the urge to pound the fuck out of me.

"Fuck, baby, you feel so good," he groaned, his breaths coming heavily.

"I'm good, move." Fuck, I needed him to move.

"It's not going to be slow. I'm too worked up for that. I need you so bad," he warned.

"Fuck me hard and deep. Make me yours." Slow and gentle was the last thing I wanted right now.

Xavier didn't need to be told twice. He didn't waste any time before he pulled back a little, angled his hips, and slammed back in, nailing my sweet spot dead on. I gave a small scream as the electric jolt of pleasure shot through me.

"Oh, I love that sound," Xavier moaned as he picked up his pace.

I wrapped my legs around his hips and my hands made their way down Xavier's back to his ass. I dug my fingernails into his butt cheeks, and was rewarded with a deep moan. He continued to pound into me hard and deep, hitting my prostate with every thrust.

I could feel that he was getting closer as his cock was getting harder. Xavier moved his free hand down to my hard and leaking cock. He started to jerk me off in time with his thrusts. I was a moaning mess as the pleasure soared through me. I felt like I was floating on air and I didn't want it to end.

After another direct hit to my sweet spot, I screamed his name as I came hard all over his hand. The tightening of my walls was enough to push Xavier over the edge and he exploded deep inside of my ass.

I moaned as I felt Xavier's hot cum filling me up inside. The heat from his cum coating my walls was unlike anything I had ever felt before. I could feel Xavier's cock pulsing and it caused my own cock to twitch a couple more times, dripping more beads of cum down Xavier's hand.

Both of us were breathing heavily, but I reached down and grabbed Xavier's hand and brought it up to my mouth. I ran my tongue along his hand, getting my cum off of it. Xavier moaned as he watched me lick my own cum off each and every one of his fingers until it was all gone.

Xavier bent down and pressed his lips against mine in a heated kiss. He shoved his tongue into my mouth, sucking on my tongue to get the sweet taste of my cum in his own mouth. I moaned and easily gave myself up to Xavier.

Xavier broke the kiss when the need for oxygen became too much for the both of us.

"Fuck, I'm never letting you get off this bed," he growled.

"I got some handcuffs in the bedside drawer," I said, flashing him a playful grin. We had a lot of time to make up for and I planned to take advantage of every single second he was here.

Xavier reached over and pulled out the cuffs. He had them dangling from one finger as his eyes found mine and he spoke. "Fuck, I love you."

"I love you too."

I had no idea what was going to happen in the future, but I didn't care. Because as long as Xavier was in my life, then I knew we would work it out. We loved each other and I couldn't wait to see what the future had in store for us.

Thank you for reading Gage and Xavier's story.

For more the Smokejumpers series, you can find Jackson at your favorite online retailer.

If you enjoyed this book, please return to your favorite retailer and leave a review. Even a few words could mean the world to an author.

Hey everyone!
I've a new series for you to check out next!

If you enjoy small town yuMMy man love—and let's face it, who doesn't?—be sure you snag your copy. This one is a little less gritty and dark than my other books have been, but it has more of that delicious gay male romance we all love to fall into. Join me and find your favorite book boyfriend in _Cade_, Book 1 in the Jasper Springs series.

Turn the page to read the blurb! ☺

Home is where the heart is...

Life in Jasper Springs may look perfect, but for Cade Green there's one thing still missing... a hunky billionaire to whisk him away, just like in the movies he can't stop binge watching after his latest break up. But life isn't some romantic tale for guys like him. That is, until the man of his dreams shows up at the local bar's karaoke night.

Can Cade's small-town heart handle the whirlwind that Weston brings?

Famed bachelor Weston Rhodes reluctantly returns to his hometown, planning on nothing more than a fleeting visit. The last thing he expects to find is a reason to stay. However, after one intense night, he soon discovers himself falling for the small town's adorable veterinarian. Can Weston, used to city lights and endless possibilities, embrace a fairy-tale romance in his quaint hometown?

Readers seeking a small town good boy/bad boy billionaire, opposites attract romance set in a cozy little town may find this story hits those buttons.
While Cade and Weston may have cameos in future stories, each book in this series can be read as a standalone.

Grab Cade here:
https://books2read.com/JasperSprings1

OTHER BOOKS BY EVIE

Federal Protection Agency
Mason
Rafe
Ryzen
Cooper
Noah
Damien
Sebastian
Gabe
Logan

Ruthless Empire
Courting Danger
Chasing Danger
Kissing Danger

Smokejumpers
Hawke
Cyrus
Jase
Gage
Jackson
Xavier

EVIE RILEY

Jasper Springs
Cade
Dawson
Drew
Grayson
Riley
Mitch

From The Edge
Shattered
Runaway
Jaded
Rescue
Hidden
Tormented

Gray Vale Pack
His Fated Mate
His Wounded Warrior
His Healing Heart

ABOUT THE AUTHOR

Evie Riley is a prolific, neurodivergent author known for her captivating MM romance novels. She has gained a significant following and topped the LGBT+ action and adventure bestseller charts with her series.

Evie's writing style often explores dark and gritty themes where her men must overcome difficult obstacles in their search for love, but she has also ventured into sweeter small-town romances, incorporating tropes like enemies-to-lovers, friends-to-lovers, age-gap, and forced proximity. She is known for crafting engaging romantic suspense novels and has a knack for creating interconnected series worlds that keep readers invested.

Interestingly, Ms. Riley has hinted at exploring new genres, such as Alien Omegaverse Romance, in the future.

Outside of writing, she enjoys spending time at the beach and has a quirky personality, described by her partner as ranging from cute to deadly, depending on her blood-chocolate levels.

Evie spends her nights writing bad boys in love, and her days wrangling the sweet boys she loves.